CONSORT OF REBELS

MAGIC AWAKENED #3

SADIE MOSS

For More Information:
www.SadieMossAuthor.com

For updates on new releases, promotions, and giveaways, sign up for my
MAILING LIST.

CHAPTER 1

THREE SMALL SLIVERS of light cut across the dark floor.

They disappeared momentarily as I blinked my eyes shut, my heavy lids unwilling to rise again.

I dragged them open, forced my eyes back into focus.

Stared at the three narrow lines of yellow light.

Ten days. That's how long I'd been stuck in this fucking dungeon cell.

Or maybe it was seven... or fourteen... or twenty. I had no natural light to judge by and couldn't tell when the sun rose or set. I'd been trying to keep count of the meals Kate brought me, but her visits didn't seem to come at regular intervals, and I was pretty sure if she found me sleeping, sometimes she just left without delivering any food or water. That would explain why I felt so weak.

Then again, several things could explain that.

I was underfed, hadn't slept more than a few hours at a time in days, and had festering injuries from the fight with Christine and her Touched backup at the warehouse in the Outskirts.

My magic was also still suppressed. But even without being able to feel the flicker of power deep in my belly, I could tell somehow that it was agitated, searching for the four men it was bonded to. If it wasn't repressed, it probably would've exploded all over this little cell by now. That seemed to be its usual reaction to stress.

The three sharp lines of light on the floor flickered again. But this time it wasn't because of my drooping eyelids.

A figure had passed in front of the door.

My head cleared a little, becoming more alert as I strained my ears. The effort of focusing caused a headache to flare like a starburst in my brain, but I ignored the throbbing pain and lifted my eyes to the tiny window in the solid wood door of my cell. Two thick metal bars spanned the small window vertically, and the light peeking around them cast the three long lines on the floor.

"How is she?"

It was Rain. I'd recognize that fucker's raspy voice in my sleep by now. In fact, I heard it in my sleep almost every time I managed to doze off. He'd supplanted my father in my dreams, starring in pretty much all my nightmares now.

Just another reason I wanted to kill the asshole.

"Weak, but alive," another voice answered. Softer. Female. Kate.

"Good. Keep her that way. I'm almost ready to perform the magic pull on her, and she's no use to me dead."

"Yes, sir."

I scoffed under my breath. *No use to him dead.* Not until he'd stolen my magic anyway. Then I had a feeling my usefulness, dead or alive, would plummet to less than zero.

That had to be why he hadn't bothered healing my wounds or

even bandaging them. Why he hadn't given me clothes or a blanket to ward off the cold that permeated the stone walls of my cell. Once he was done with me, he'd either kill me or let me die.

I thought back to Gerald's slack face and half-focused eyes the day I ran into him on the palace steps, and a shiver ran down my spine. If that was what I had to look forward to after Rain pulled the magic from my body, maybe I'd prefer death after all.

No. Don't think like that, Lana. Remember your promise.

The day Rain captured me, before he'd knocked me out and moved me from the large room with the metal cage into this dungeon, I'd made a vow to myself. I'd promised I would make it back to my four alive.

I could picture each of them as clearly as if they were here in this room with me, and the thought of them simultaneously soothed my soul and sent a piercing pain through my heart. My abduction would be driving them out of their minds with worry. What were they doing now? Were they trying to find me? But how could they? They had no idea Rain was behind any of this.

All they knew was that Christine, the Resistance's ex-leader, had turned traitor. The trap we'd set to prove her guilt had worked—maybe a little too well. She'd both proven and expanded upon her betrayal, using a transport spell to drag me away to Rain's secret hideout. The last memories I had of Jae, Akio, Fenris, and Corin were the looks of stark terror on their faces as they watched the swirling purple smoke of the transport spell envelop me.

The thought turned my stomach, and I shoved it out of my head.

You'll find a way to get back to them. Don't give up.

The weak inner voice of my flickering optimism was interrupted when a face came into view outside the door.

3

"It won't be long now, Miss Lockwood. The spell takes a week to recharge between uses, but it's nearly ready. I apologize for the delay, but there was another mage who arrived before you, and his health was declining, so...."

Rain trailed off, his shoulder lifting in a shrug. He was silhouetted against the light, so I could barely make out his features. I wasn't sure he could see me at all where I sat huddled against the wall in the corner, but I sent a scathing glare his way just in case he could.

Ugh. The fucking Gifted. Why did they have to be so godsdamned *polite* about everything? As if apologizing for the delay made what he planned to do any less sinister. As if wearing the veneer of civility made him anything but a monster.

"Go fuck yourself, Rain."

My voice was rough and weak from days of disuse, but at least my words were honest.

He sighed dramatically. "You have such a strong spirit. It's truly a shame you won't even consider joining me. You could keep your magic. And I could use someone like you by my side." He turned his head slightly, and the yellow light behind him picked up the streaks of silvery gray in his hair, giving him the world's most ironic halo. "But then again, I'd never really be able to trust you, would I?"

"You can trust I'm going to kill you."

That was the other promise I'd made the day he captured me.

And I intended to keep it.

Rain sighed again, like a father sick of hearing the same far-fetched story from a child with an overactive imagination. He turned away from the door to address Kate. "Prepare the machine. When I get back from the palace tonight, we'll get started."

4

"Yes, sir."

Her voice was soft and deferential when she addressed him. The few times she'd spoken to me, it'd been sharp and cruel. I wasn't sure exactly how she got involved in all of this, but she seemed to regard Rain as some kind of savior or prophet. He'd probably brainwashed her with talk of his insane vision for the future, a world in which only a few "worthy" souls possessed magic and ruled like gods over those who didn't.

And that was assuming the Gifted and Touched actually *survived* his second attempt at a large-scale magic pull. They hadn't the first time.

Rain shot me one last glance before turning and walking away.

The three slivers of light spread across the floor in front of me again. I stared at them as Kate's footsteps retreated in the opposite direction.

Was she headed off to prepare the "machine?" What did that even mean? I assumed it was part of the process of extracting magic from a living being, something that shouldn't even be possible. It brought to mind images of medieval torture racks with huge gears that squealed and grated as they turned.

My stomach twisted then grumbled. Experiencing nausea and biting hunger at the same time was confusing and unpleasant, each sensation only exacerbating the other.

But maybe Kate was a little more worried than she'd let on about fulfilling Rain's directive to keep me alive, because she returned to my cell a few moments later.

The door cracked open several inches, and a thin, olive-skinned hand reached in to deposit a bowl on the floor. Steam rose from it in lazy spirals, carrying with it the aroma of chicken and rice. At the scent, my hunger won out, and I crawled forward as soon as the door thudded shut.

I could feel her eyes on me, peering down to watch me as I stuffed handfuls of food into my mouth, but I ignored her. With a slightly fuller belly, I crawled back toward the opposite corner. As I crossed the room, she cracked the door again, slipping her hand in to retrieve the empty dish.

The first few days I'd been here, she'd made a point to only open the door when I was as far away from it as possible. But she didn't seem to care as much about that now—probably due to the fact that I looked like absolute shit. Hell, I wouldn't have been intimidated by myself right now either.

In addition to the bite wound on my shoulder, which had turned an ugly purple color and continued to seep blood, I had several other scrapes and bruises. All of it could've been healed with a potion or spell, but Rain didn't seem interested in wasting magic on me. He'd also refused to give me anything to cover up with after my forced shift from wolf to human had left me in only pants, my empty dagger sheaths, one boot, and a bra.

If he was trying to play some kind of mind game with me, to make me feel weak and exposed without half my clothes, then the joke was on him. I didn't give a fuck about decency—at least, not over the more pressing concern of staying alive.

Still, I would've killed for a godsdamned shirt. The stone walls of this dungeon cell were always cold and a little bit damp, and after days of goose bumps constantly covering my body, my skin was painful to touch.

"It will be over soon," Kate muttered quietly.

I wasn't sure if she was trying to reassure me or threaten me. Or maybe she was talking to herself.

Not for the first time, I wondered what Rain had promised

her in exchange for her help. Couldn't she see that whatever carrot he'd dangled in front of her was a lie?

Hell, Kate had been the one to kill Christine once the Resistance leader was no longer useful to Rain. Why didn't she understand that to him, people were either tools to be used or impediments to be gotten rid of? Did she truly expect him to keep his word about whatever reward he'd promised her?

I curled up into a ball on the rough, dirty floor, trying to generate a small bubble of body heat. After a few moments, Kate's footsteps padded away again. This time, she didn't return.

Weariness tugged at me, the weights on my eyelids pulling them closed even as the cold seeping into me tensed all my muscles. I wished desperately for the little flame of magic inside me to burst back to life, to warm my body and heal my injuries.

But it didn't.

I allowed myself to lie there for a few moments, breathing steadily, letting the food settle in my stomach and give me strength.

Just like I had that day on the mountain with Fen, I imagined myself as a wolf, told myself *that* was my true form, not this human one. I envisioned my heavy paws thudding against the earth. My teeth snapping, piercing flesh and bone. My hackles rising as a growl rumbled in my throat.

The shift to wolf form didn't happen, of course. The magic wouldn't work inside this cell. But the images bolstered me anyway, reminding me that even if I couldn't access that part of myself right now, it was still in there. There was more to me than met the eye.

I was wolf.

I was mage.

I was demon.

I was human.

And despite the old family name Rain had addressed me by earlier, I was *Lana fucking Crow.*

It was time to show him and his lackey bitch exactly what that meant.

Forcing my eyelids open, I sat back up, a wave of dizziness passing over me as I did. I gritted my teeth, pressing against the wall for support and leverage as I rose slowly to my feet. Me knees tried to buckle, but I locked them until the spots stopped dancing before my eyes.

My plan of escape was a long shot at best, a hopeless fantasy at worst. But I was out of time to come up with a better option.

If I was still here when Rain got back tonight, I'd be worse than dead.

CHAPTER 2

WHEN MY LEGS felt steady enough, I let go of the wall and reached for the sheaths strapped to my thighs. The one upside of Rain not offering me a change of clothes was that he also hadn't bothered to take these.

They were empty. I'd tried to stab him in the heart with one of my daggers and thrown the other at his head when he first captured me. The blades were enchanted to materialize back in their sheaths so I'd never lose them, but of course that spell wouldn't work in this fucking magic suppressing cell.

But it *should* still work outside this room.

Carefully, I undid the buckles and removed the sheaths from my legs. Wrapping the straps tight around one hand, I crept toward the door and peered through the little window. Other cells lined the large, empty stone room, similar to mine. Wall sconces holding glowing yellow orbs of magical light were spaced along the walls in between the wooden cell doors.

There was no sign of Kate.

She and Rain were the only two people I'd seen or heard since

I arrived, but I wasn't sure whether that meant they were the only ones here. Maybe he had other guards outside this room. I had no idea what the layout of this place was, other than the tiny area I could see from inside my cell.

I couldn't worry about that now though. First things first.

Grimacing in anticipation, I slid my hand between the bars on my cell door. The window was at an awkward height, the bottom of it just reaching my chin, so I had to lean up against the door to get my arm through. As soon as I touched the rough wood of the door and the smooth metal of the bars, agony burned through me.

They were enchanted with the same pain spell that had been on the metal cage he dropped on me—a simple but effective deterrent to keep prisoners from attacking the doors of their cells.

Effective for anybody less stupid and determined than me, anyway.

Sucking in ragged breaths through clenched teeth, I pressed closer to the door, forcing my elbow and bicep through the tight space between the bars. The pain was most intense anywhere I made contact with the door, but it quickly spread through my entire body like air filling up a balloon.

Come on, you stupid things. Work. Work!

When my arm was as far through the opening as I could push it, I held up the empty sheaths like an offering to the gods, praying desperately as my hand shook like a leaf.

I'd tried this once before, right after I arrived here. It hadn't worked. After a few minutes, the pain had grown so intense I'd been afraid I would drop the sheaths, and I'd pulled my arm back, shivering and sweating.

My theory was that, because of the strength of the magic

suppressing spell on this little room, I'd need to get the sheaths as far away from the cell as possible for as long as possible to give the enchantment on the daggers a chance of working.

Or maybe the enchantment had been broken entirely when the sheaths were brought into a magic repressing cell.

Maybe I was sticking these fucking things out the window for no reason, weakening myself further on the basis of a stupid, empty hope.

Not. Helping! I scolded myself, baring my teeth against the cry that wanted to burst from my throat. I couldn't let it. I couldn't do anything that might draw Kate back here.

My hand shook with the effort of holding the sheaths out, and my legs went weak, causing more of my body to press against the door. Agony tore through me as if my muscles were separating, pulling apart from my bones and trying to escape the confines of my skin.

Coherent thought became difficult as the pain overtook me, seeping into my mind like poison. Twice, instinct took over and attempted to pull me away from the door, but I fought it down, pressing my body harder to the rough wood instead. My skin was slick with sweat, fat drops of it trickling down my bare arms, neck, and back, mixing with the blood seeping from my shoulder wound.

Blackness edged my vision, and my hand outside the cell started to droop, the effort of keeping it raised becoming too great. It felt like I was holding a lead weight instead of empty leather sheaths.

Wait....

My eyes snapped open, and I shook my head to focus my vision. I peered blearily through the cell window. Tears pricked my eyes, and I let out a small, gasping laugh.

11

Not lead weights. Daggers.

The two blades had reappeared inside their sheaths.

I resisted the urge to yank my arm back, not wanting to risk dropping or dislodging the weapons. Instead, I slowly pulled them through the bars, stepping away from the door as I did so. As soon as my arm cleared the window, I fell backward onto my butt, bruising my tailbone and bumping the back of my head on the hard stone floor.

Not that it fucking mattered.

After the agony of cozying up to that damn door, a couple bruises felt like butterfly kisses.

And I had my daggers back.

Too weak to stand again, I crawled back over to the corner out of the light and strapped the sheaths back to my thighs. The effect was more comforting than a warm blanket.

Propping my back against the chilly stone wall, I settled in to wait.

FORTUNATELY, today wasn't one of those days Kate decided to let me skip a meal. A few hours later, my ears perked at the sound of soft footsteps approaching my cell. I stiffened, pressing farther back into the shadows of the corner. I was almost certain she wouldn't notice the daggers I now wore in my sheaths, but my heart thudded heavily in my chest anyway.

When the dark-haired woman appeared outside my cell, I glanced wanly up at her like I always did. After casting a critical eye in my direction, Kate disappeared from the window, and the lock on the door opened with a click. She set down a small tray with a bowl and a jug of water and shut the door behind her.

Just like I had this morning—or whatever time it had been—I crawled on hands and knees over to the meager sustenance. Pride urged me to stand, but I wasn't going to use my dwindling reserves of strength until I had to. And I'd be a fool to turn down the last meal I might get for a while.

She peered down at me through the little window while I ate, and I made sure to stay away from the light creeping through the window, pressing myself close to the wall by the door.

When I finished, I let out a satisfied sigh, sucking in a deep lungful of air. I lingered for a moment, dabbing up the last few pieces of rice with one finger as I tried to get my brain and body to sync up. My mind felt more alert as nerves and adrenaline sharpened my senses, but my body still felt weak and sluggish, like it lagged two steps behind.

Finally, unable to put it off any longer, I set the dish down on the tray and turned, crawling slowly back toward the far corner.

When I was halfway across the room, the door opened behind me. The dishes on the tray rattled as Kate picked them up.

And I moved.

Pivoting on one knee and pushing off the ball of my back foot, I leapt toward the door. I slid one of my daggers smoothly out of its sheath as I did, reaching out with my other hand to grab Kate's wrist.

I yanked, and the tray went flying. The jug and bowl shattered with a loud crash as I pulled Kate into the room, throwing myself on top of her and pressing the dagger to her throat.

In the quiet after the crash, Kate's sharp breaths pierced the air. She opened her mouth to make another noise, but I bore down harder with my blade, drawing a thin red line across her neck.

"Don't scream," I whispered. "Or it'll be the last thing you do."

Her nostrils flared, disgust and rage flickering across her features in the dim light.

Then she opened her mouth and screamed.

The action made the dagger dig deeper into her neck, and blood welled. I pulled back in surprise, and in that second, I saw a glint of triumph in her eye.

This fucking bitch called my bluff.

I barely had time to process the thought before she bucked her hips, throwing me off balance and rolling to dislodge me.

Kate scrambled for the door. I dove after her, grabbing her by the ankle. She kicked out with her other foot, catching my cheekbone.

Stars burst in my vision as pain exploded in my skull.

She reached for the still-open door, and I gave up trying to pull her back. Instead, I let go and darted past her, slamming into the door just as she tried to escape the room. Agony flared in my body. The heavy wood smashed into her fingers, which were braced against the frame. She let out another scream, more piercing than the first.

Fuck. If anybody else was in this building, they must've heard the commotion by now.

I shoved Kate backward and kicked the door all the way shut, rounding on her. She cradled her broken fingers to her chest, wild hazel eyes fixed on me. When I advanced toward her, she feinted and tried to dodge around me, but I slashed out with my dagger, catching her across the shoulder.

She stumbled, and I pressed my advantage, driving her into the wall and using my bodyweight to keep her there. I drew my other dagger, crisscrossing the blades over her neck.

"Okay, you got me," I panted, trying to slow my breathing so she wouldn't know how winded I was already. "I didn't want to kill you. I still don't. Hell, I *should*. I should slit your throat right now for what you did to Christine, and for whatever else you've done for Rain. But I'm sick of people fucking dying because of me."

"I am prepared to die for him." Her shoulder glistened with blood, and her neck was smeared with red from her previous encounter with my dagger, but her voice was confident and strong.

"Yeah? What'd he promise you, huh?" I dug my blades a little deeper into her skin, but I hadn't been lying. I was sick of all the death that seemed to follow me around. I was sick of trying to justify the lives I'd taken. "Your very own worshippers and slaves, once you have enough magic to live like a god? You realize he'd just as soon kill you as give you any of that, right?"

"He has already *saved* my life," Kate hissed, her dark eyes burning with fervor. "His vision is the only way, the only future. No one sees the world like Rain Blackshear does."

"Thank fuck for that."

Stepping back quickly, I raised my right hand and bashed the butt of my dagger against Kate's temple. She pitched to the side, eyes rolling up into her head.

As soon as she was down, I sheathed my blades and bent over with my hands on my knees, weakness flooding my body like ice water. The adrenaline of the fight had helped keep me upright, but my strength was flagging badly. I needed to get out of here before Rain came back or someone else came to investigate the noise. I didn't have too many more fights left in me.

Crouching down beside Kate's prone form, I pulled her shirt off. One sleeve was sticky with blood, and I cut it off before slipping the rest of the garment over my head. I had no idea where I was, but if—no, *when*—I made it out of here, I'd have a better chance of surviving if I was protected from the elements.

Her feet were a bit bigger than mine, and her boot had a slight heel where mine didn't, but I'd rather walk funny than walk barefoot. I yanked her left shoe off and shoved it on my foot.

A quick pat down revealed nothing else useful on her but a small key ring.

I used the blood-soaked sleeve to bind her wrists, wincing at the purple, swollen fingers on her right hand. But I forced down my pity. Kate had killed Christine. She was helping Rain carry out his insane plan, and she'd treated me horribly as a prisoner. I might not be able to bring myself to kill her in cold blood, but that didn't mean she deserved to live.

Slipping out of the cell, I glanced around cautiously. The large room was still empty. Two hallways led away from it in different directions. One of them I'd been able to see from inside the cell, and one I hadn't.

I turned back to the door of my cell and tried several keys until I found the one that locked it. Shoving the key ring in my pocket, I crept toward the newly revealed hallway.

But before I made it three steps, heat and power flared in my belly, almost bringing me to my knees.

Oh, shit.

My magic was back.

And it was pissed.

CHAPTER 3

ALL THE POWER that had been suppressed by Rain's prison cell flowed through my veins like liquid lightning, overwhelming me.

I glanced down at myself, almost expecting to find light emanating from my skin, but all I saw was a body covered in sweat, grime, and smears of blood. My bra, which had once been black, was now tinged a brownish gray, and my usually flame-red hair was about the same color as my bra.

But I could feel the magic burning inside me, straining to reconnect to the bonds it had forged with my four. I pressed a hand against the wall to stay upright, willing it to calm the fuck down.

Not right now. Please, gods, not right now.

I wished I could explain to the power raging through me that I was *trying* to find my way back to my men; I just needed it to behave for a little while longer so I could do that.

Keeping my hand on the stone wall for stability, I stumbled down the long hallway. It was carved right out of the rock and was obviously made more for function than form. The walls were rough and uneven, and the sconces jutting out were spaced far enough apart that the hall lapsed into darkness between them.

I summoned a small flame above my free hand, both for the added light and as a precautionary measure, in case I ran into other residents or guards. My ears stayed perked for any threat, but the only sounds were my short breaths and the shuffling of my feet.

The stillness was eerie.

Shit. Maybe Rain and Kate were the only two people in the world who knew about this place, whatever and wherever it was.

That wouldn't surprise me. Rain could've easily hired some Touched goons to guard his lair, but he struck me as paranoid enough not to trust anyone but Kate with the knowledge of what he was doing here. That must be the reason he'd been able to keep his responsibility for the Great Death a secret all these years.

He told my father about his plans once. And my dad tried to stop him.

Pride and grief swelled inside me in equal measure at the thought. Rain had probably learned his lesson about revealing his sick secrets after that.

I followed several winding stone corridors, all of which looked exactly the same. When I turned down a new hallway, hope made my heart pound faster. A door stood at the end of it.

Picking up my pace, I half shuffled, half ran toward the large wooden door. But I slowed as I neared it, noticing the blue glow that pulsed over the dark wood.

Warded.

Fuck.

It made sense. If Rain didn't have guards watching over this place, he must've locked it down tight with magical protections instead.

Godsdamn it. Guards, I could fight—or charm. Magical wards, on the other hand... I had no way around those. Growling, I turned around and retraced my steps through the catacombs, pushing through my bone-deep weariness.

Trying to keep a mental map of which hallways I'd already ventured down, I kept moving, stumbling upon two more warded doors.

By the time I reached a third one, panic was whipping my magic up into a frenzy. This place was fucking huge. Even if no one stopped me, I could spend hours wandering the stone halls fruitlessly, searching for a way out that may not even exist.

I turned and shuffled back the way I'd come, the vibrating tension of my magic at odds with the dwindling strength of my body. Choosing another random offshoot, I ventured down the dark corridor, fingers brushing the cold wall.

A grinding sound up ahead stopped me in my tracks.

Fuck. Maybe there *was* somebody else here.

I peered down the dimly lit hallway, muscles tensed. The grinding sound grew louder, but I still couldn't see anything.

Suddenly, a man stepped right out of the wall before me.

No. Not a man. A part of the stone.

The creature had no features, just a blank face. And it was bigger than most humans, seven feet tall at least. It's head almost scraped the low ceiling of the cavernous tunnel.

For a second, I just stared at it, dumbfounded.

Then the grating sound came again, and another creature just like the first emerged from the wall behind me.

They moved simultaneously, faster than rock had a right to. Two large, rough fists swung for me.

I ducked too late. The fist meant for my face missed me, but the one aimed at my midsection hit me in the shoulder instead, sending me flying into the wall. The bite wound on my shoulder sang with pain as I slipped under another rocky fist, darting down the hallway.

Raising both hands, I turned around as the two creatures barreled toward me. Flame shot from my palms, sending a scorching fireball careening through the cavern. Heat enveloped me, and I swore I could hear a few strands of my hair sizzle.

Shit. Too much! My magic raged under the surface of my skin, barely under my control.

And it didn't even slow the rock creatures down at all. They emerged from the billowing flame unscathed, expressionless faces trained on me.

I fell backward, and a second after I hit the ground, a large stone knee landed by my side. One of the figures knelt over me, and I twisted my head just in time to avoid having my face crushed by its large fist.

Usually, I liked close-quarter fighting. I was good with my fists and my blades. But neither of those would work against this big motherfucker and his friend.

Scrabbling backward like a crab, I threw my hands out again, calling on the power of wind. My magic surged through me, and this time I didn't try to stop it, didn't try to control it. I let the wind shriek through the tunnel, my own scream lost in the howling noise.

The stone men dug their feet in, pushing into the violent gust, but it pressed them back.

I couldn't sustain it forever though. When they were a few yards away from me, I let the wind drop and did the best thing I could think of when faced with magical stone adversaries. I ran.

My mismatched shoes made my gate uneven, and I careened between the walls like a drunk trying to run an obstacle course. But I kept moving, even as the thundering sound of footsteps grew louder behind me.

When the corridor I was in opened up into a large room, I sprinted inside—and the footsteps behind me stopped.

I whirled around. The two figures stood stock-still just outside the entryway to the room. Then, without a sound, they stepped back to the walls, disappearing into the stone.

Why didn't they follow me in here?

Backing slowly away from the door, I edged farther into the room, and then glanced around at the new space I had entered.

I gasped.

It was cavernous, at least three stories tall. I had entered in the middle level, onto a balcony that surrounded the perimeter of the room. Below me, a steel platform ten feet across took up the center of the floor. Six large prongs rose from it, looking almost like the setting on a gigantic ring.

Except there was no diamond set inside these prongs. Instead, they held a shifting ball of bright white light.

It pulsed with power, the energy radiating from it nearly knocking me off my feet.

Magic.

This was what Rain had stolen.

I blinked back tears as I stared down at it, overwhelmed by the otherworldly beauty of the bright, shifting light. It was pure, concentrated magic, burning like a star.

A staircase led from the balcony to the main floor, and I crept down it, gaze locked on the magic star. From up close, it looked even bigger and felt more powerful. I swore I could hear a low hum coming from it, as if the concentrated magic were alive.

But Rain couldn't use this magic, could he? If he'd gotten this from his first magic pull, it was inaccessible to him. Or so he'd told me.

Thank the gods. Because if he had access to this much power, he'd be unstoppable.

The thought hardly comforted me. His plans for a second magic pull were well underway, and he seemed confident that this time, he *would* be able to use the magic he stole from others.

I had to stop him.

But first, I had to get the fuck out of here.

The room was quiet. I shot a glance up at the balcony level, but the stone figures hadn't reappeared. Were there more of them guarding the corridors on this level? I wasn't sure I could survive another encounter with them.

But I couldn't give up trying to find a way out. It'd been hours since Rain left for the Capital; he might be back any minute. And as soon as he found Kate tied up in my old cell, he'd realize what I'd done and hunt me down.

Several corridors led away from the main level of this room. Stealing one last look back at the ball of magic suspended within the metal prongs, I picked a passage at random and darted cautiously down it. The hallways down here were darker than the ones above, with cobwebs draping across them in places. Although no creatures emerged from the walls, I hit two more dead ends at warded doors, and my jaw began to ache from being clenched so tight.

But the next door I stumbled upon wasn't warded. It wasn't even locked.

It hung slightly ajar, and somehow that sight made me more nervous than all those pulsing blue wards had.

This wasn't right. Rain would never be so careless.

Was he back already? Had he come through here? Did he know I was down here too?

Slowly, tentatively, I reached for the door. It creaked as I pushed it open, and I winced. The area beyond was swallowed up in darkness.

I braced myself and was about to step through when a noise drew my attention. A muffled voice came from another corridor that intercepted this one several yards behind me.

I froze, torn by indecision. Should I step into the blackness beyond and into a possible trap? Or should I turn and fight Rain now—maybe even get the jump on him? I was weak, but the magic that burned inside me was still raging out of control. And it was pulling me back toward the sound of the voice, probably itching for a fight.

Decision made, I slipped a dagger from my sheath. I kept one hand free for spell casting but didn't summon a flame yet. The light would give away my position too soon.

Turning, I crept silently down the corridor. I pressed myself to the wall near the intersecting hallway, listening intently. Whoever it was had gone quiet, but the sound of breathing met my ears. Coming closer.

Bursting around the corner, I darted into the hall, raising my dagger at the same time I summoned a ball of flame above my other hand.

The fire flared in the darkness, almost blinding in its brightness. The man before me grunted, raising his forearm to block my strike. He swept his arm up and around, wrapping his other hand around the back of my fist to control the dagger.

"We really have to stop meeting like this, kitten," he drawled.

My blade clattered to the ground.

"*Akio?*"

CHAPTER 4

THE INCUBUS'S dark eyes glittered in the light of the fire that still burned above my raised palm.

"Hello, Lana."

I stared at him as he spoke my name, a million questions burning on the tip of my tongue. What was he doing here? Where were the others? How had they found me?

But none of those thoughts made it past my lips. I was frozen in place, held captive by the sight of his angular features, his deeply tanned skin, and his jet-black hair. I'd often thought Akio looked like a god, but in this shadowy hallway, illuminated only by the dancing glow of my flame, he looked like exactly what he was—a demon.

The best fucking kind of demon.

Emotions too powerful to name slammed into me, making my breath hitch. I realized for the first time that I *hadn't* truly expected to make it out of here alive, hadn't expected to ever see my four again. And coming face-to-face with Akio like this left me reeling.

I didn't think. I wasn't even aware of moving until the flame above my palm abruptly snuffed out and I found myself pressed flush against him, my lips seeking his in the sudden darkness.

He stiffened with surprise when my mouth crashed into his, but then his body softened against mine, his lips warm and smooth as silk. The unique, spicy scent that was all Akio surrounded me, filling my nostrils as I wrapped my arms around him, devouring him with my kiss.

A sound almost like a purr rolled through his chest when our tongues met, and my legs went weak.

"Akio!" a whispered voice called urgently in the dark. A blue-white glow filled the corridor several yards away.

He tensed again, his hands on my hips stiffening, and I suddenly realized what we were doing. I wrenched my lips away from his and stepped back, embarrassed, though I wasn't sure why.

Maybe it was because our relationship had never really been one of overt affection.

Or maybe it was because despite my injuries and exhaustion, despite the danger of our situation, all I wanted was to keep kissing him until the sun burned out.

The incubus's gaze was inscrutable in the dim blue light. He licked his lips, and I was sure he tasted mine on them. I sucked my own bottom lip into my mouth, biting it hard to keep from throwing myself into his arms again.

Before I had to think of something to say, Corin's low voice echoed down the hall.

"Lana? *Lana!*"

The blond man strode toward us quickly, a look of almost pained determination on his face, and I vaguely registered two other figures behind him before he enveloped me in his arms. His large, muscular body was warm against mine, and I could feel his heart hammering against my chest. He showered my face and mouth with kisses, not seeming to care that I was covered in sweat and grime.

"We found you. Thank the gods, we found you."

He pulled back just enough to look into my eyes. His blue irises glittered as he bent to claim my lips again in a kiss that was soft and deep.

With every breath I took, every moment our mouths were connected, my soul knit itself back together a little bit more, the magic inside me settling back down into a happy, warm glow.

Jae and Fenris approached and stood nearby. I could feel their presence down to my bones, like a soothing balm applied to fresh wounds.

I hadn't realized how broken I was until I became whole again.

Fen waited with more patience than I would've expected from him, but when Corin showed no signs of letting me go anytime soon, the wolf shifter tugged on my arm.

"Gimme."

That was all he said, and Corin reluctantly released his hold on me.

I expected Fen to kiss me too, but instead he pulled me into a crushing grip and buried his face in my hair. He sucked in deep drags of air, like he was trying to absorb my very essence. His large body shuddered in my arms, and he kept murmuring, "Fuck, killer. Fuck," over and over.

The raw pain in his voice brought tears to my eyes, and I stroked the back of his shaggy hair, trying to soothe him.

"I'm okay. It's okay."

He finally pulled his face away from my hair and pressed his forehead to mine. His chocolate brown eyes were dark pools in the dim light.

"I love you so fucking much, Lana."

The tears that had been hovering in my eyes spilled over at that, and I leaned into him to kiss his lips. The scruff on his cheeks scratched my face, sending shivers down my spine.

"I love you back, Fen," I whispered. "So fucking much."

The light beside us flared a little brighter. I looked over at Jae. Fenris let go of me, and I stepped hesitantly toward the mage. His elegant features were smooth, but his emerald eyes blazed like fire. He stepped slowly toward me, seeming as unsure as I was about what to do next.

One long-fingered hand reached out to stroke my cheek, and I unconsciously leaned into his touch like a cat. He cupped the side of my face, the cool contact of his palm making me feel unaccountably warm.

"Are you all right?" Worry wrinkled his brow as he took in my appearance.

"Yeah." I smiled.

The movement made the bruise on my cheekbone from Kate's face kick throb like a son of a bitch, but I *was* okay.

Now.

Jae started to drop his hand, but I reached up to grab it, lacing our fingers together and holding them to my chest, just under my collarbone. I wasn't ready to let our contact go yet.

My gaze flickered around the group of men huddling in the cramped tunnel with me as my brain slowly came to grips with the fact that this wasn't a dream. "What... what are you all doing here?"

"We came to rescue you," Fen answered. "I didn't think we'd find you so quick though. What were you doing?"

"I rescued myself."

He grinned wolfishly, looking more like his usual self, though his voice was still strained with worry. "Fuck yeah, you did."

"I couldn't find a door that wasn't warded though. The open one at the end of the corridor, was that you guys?"

"Yes. We brought a powerful spell stripper. We weren't sure what we'd find here." Jae nodded solemnly, his eyes still scanning me. I had a feeling he was cataloguing every one of my injuries, his concern growing with each new cut or bruise he noted.

If he wanted to heal me, I would gladly accept his ministrations, but it'd have to wait until we were out of here. The five of us had already wasted way too much time on our reunion, though I couldn't regret it.

"Good. Then let's get the fuck out of here before Rain comes back."

"*Rain?*" Corin's head reared back in surprise, his eyes going wide.

"Yup," I said grimly. "He's the asshole Christine was reporting to."

"Oh shit!" Fen's voice rose. "Does that mean he knows where the Resistance headquarters is? Did she tell him?"

I shook my head. "I'm almost positive he doesn't. She told me she never gave up that information, and I think she was telling the truth. She was fucked up and did a shitty thing, but she never wanted to hurt the Resistance members. And I don't think Rain was very concerned with the Resistance, to be honest. We were the perfect scapegoat for him."

Jae's brows drew together. "Where is Christine now?"

A shudder passed through me. "Dead. He killed her after she brought me to him. And he's done worse... much worse. But there's no time to explain it all now. We need to get out of here."

28

"Hell yes to that." Fenris wrapped an arm around my waist, supporting some of my weight. "Come on, killer. Let's get you home."

I would've insisted I could walk on my own, but I really couldn't—not as fast as we needed to go anyway. And besides, I liked the feel of Fen's strong arm holding me, his solid body next to mine. So I just wrapped my hands around his middle and headed toward the door that stood slightly ajar, flanked by the rest of my men.

The inky blackness beyond the door gave way before Jae's light, revealing a narrow corridor much like the one we were in now. But when we stepped into it, I realized the walls were made of earth, not stone. The musty smell made me sneeze, which made me hiss in pain as my cheek throbbed.

We walked through the dark tunnel in silence, Jae's glowing ball of light floating ahead of us, casting all the men's faces in harsh shadows. After a few minutes, we reached another door, and Akio pushed it open.

Fresh air flooded my lungs. I sucked it in gratefully, squinting in the afternoon sunlight. It was almost hard to believe it was daytime. I'd lost track of the hours inside the windowless room where I was kept.

"Where are we?" I asked, looking up at the tall pines surrounding us.

"In the Rocky Mountains." Fen gave me a squeeze. "About ten miles south of where you and I went running that day."

I shot a glance back as we began our trek down the steep terrain. Behind us, a slab of red, lichen-covered rock rose high, and tucked into the place where it met the earthen side of the mountain was the door we'd just come through. Even now, if I didn't know exactly what I was looking for, I would've missed it.

It was well camouflaged, and I wondered how many entrances to Rain's underground compound were hidden in this area.

"Was that door warded, or the inner one?" I asked Jae.

"The inner."

I grunted. "Makes sense. Wards out here could draw attention. As it is, the entrance is almost invisible, but still protected where it counts. Rain is smart; I'll give him that."

"I can't believe it was Rain." Fen shook is head, his brown hair flopping over his forehead. "He was the only one of the Representatives who seemed at all concerned that you'd gone missing."

My eyes snapped up. "What?"

"Yeah. Jae went to the palace to find out if they were doing anything about your disappearance, and it was just business as usual there. I think most of them were glad they didn't have to deal with you anymore."

"Except Rain." Jae's face was grim. "He pulled me aside before I left. Told me he was worried about you after what happened to your grandmother and offered to help us find you. He asked if we had any clues as to your whereabouts."

"That slimy fucking asshole!" My voice rose higher than I'd meant it to, and a startled chipmunk darted out from under a bush ahead of us. I wrestled the lid back on my temper and spoke in a quieter voice. "That must be one of his signature moves. Pretend to befriend your enemy and ask for information under the guise of trying to help." I hesitated, almost missing my next step, and Fen's arm tightened around me. "Wait. How the hell did you guys find me? If you had no idea it was Rain who'd taken me, what led you up here?"

Akio shot a glance over his shoulder. He'd taken the lead in our little expedition, and he somehow looked as effortlessly graceful and sophisticated tromping down a mountain as he did wearing a suit and sipping champagne.

"You did, kitten."

His words startled me so much I actually did miss a step this time. Only Fen's grip on me and a steadying hand from Corin stopped me from tumbling down the steep incline.

"*What?*"

Fen grinned down at me. "Yeah. A few days after Christine snatched you, I started having the strongest pull toward the mountains. I thought it was just my wolf reacting to the stress, needing to blow off steam, you know? So I ignored it for a while. There wasn't time for that—we were too busy searching for you. Then Corin mentioned he noticed a pull toward the mountains, and Jae said the same. When Akio walked in and told us he felt like going for a hike, we knew something was up."

Akio looked back again, rolling his eyes, and I chuckled.

I held onto Fen tighter, and his firm stomach flexed under my hand. "But how could you all have felt a pull toward me? My magic was suppressed inside that cell. *I* couldn't even feel it."

"The magic within you was repressed," Jae confirmed, stepping up to my other side as the trees around us cleared. "But the part of your magic that exists outside of you, in each of us, wasn't. The bond has grown even stronger since it first formed, and it led us to you."

"So you just... wandered up into the mountains with a spell stripper and who knows what else, not even sure if you'd find me?"

"We knew we'd find you." Corin's firm voice came from behind me. "We had to."

My heart clenched, more glad than I could ever say that fate brought these four men into my life.

I hadn't thought I wanted magic. I hadn't thought I wanted emotional attachments—had seen them as a weakness, even. But I was finally starting to realize they could be my greatest strengths.

"Thank you," I murmured, my voice soft with emotion. "For coming for me."

Akio stopped and turned suddenly, bringing our entire troupe to a halt. His eyes glittered like dark jewels as he regarded me.

"Kitten, we will *always* come for you."

With that pronouncement, he resumed walking down the mountain, his gait smooth and controlled. I stared after him for a moment, a riot of emotions ricocheting through my chest, before Fenris tugged me gently into motion again.

We lapsed into silence for a while. My injuries and exhaustion were catching up to me, but I tried not to let them show. Jae kept shooting me worried sidelong glances, and I knew if he saw even the slightest hint that my strength was flagging, he'd insist on stopping to heal me now.

As much as I appreciated his concern, I wanted to get off this fucking mountain and back to the safety of Beatrice's house. I could've tried to heal myself as we walked, but I was pretty sure I'd definitely fall down the mountain if I did that.

By the time we reached the low foothills, where the downward slope eased into a more manageable angle and the clusters of pine and rocks were replaced by swaths of tall grass, it was impossible for me to hide my weakness any longer. Both my calves were cramping, my mouth felt like sandpaper, and the bruise on my face throbbed in time to the beat of my footsteps.

Fenris had offered to carry me, but I shook my head stubbornly. He'd only ever given me one piggyback, and I didn't want to spoil that memory with this one. But I did accept gratefully when Corin came around to my other side so the two men could support me between them.

We trekked about a quarter of a mile down a winding mountain road, and I was about to ask the guys if they'd walked all the way here from Denver, when Jae's car suddenly popped into view ahead of us. He must've put an illusion spell on it to hide it.

The mage's shiny silver vehicle was one of the most beautiful sights I'd ever seen. Mostly because it meant I wouldn't have to keep holding my body upright.

He removed the wards and unlocked it, and I clambered gratefully into the back seat. Akio and Fen climbed in on either side of me, and seconds after Jae started the car, my eyes fell shut, my head lolling on the incubus's shoulder.

I heard snippets of the men talking as we drove, discussing the new information I'd shared and what to do about it. There was more they needed to know, so much more, but no matter how badly I wanted to join in the conversation, I couldn't force my eyes open.

When the gentle movement of the car stopped and the rumbling engine cut off, my body jerked upright. I looked around quickly, trying to orient myself.

"It's okay, killer." Fen smoothed my hair back from my face. "We're here."

Behind him, through the car's window, I saw the enchanted fountain that fronted Beatrice's estate. The large drops of water-fish leapt lazily from the pool, unaware of all the turmoil the house had seen over the last few weeks.

I turned to peer out the opposite window, and gasped.

"What the hell happened to this place?"

CHAPTER 5

Fenris chuckled. "Jae happened. Do you like it?"

I shot a glance at Jae as we all piled out of the car, Fen holding my elbow to help me walk. "Were you guys under attack?"

"No." He shook his head, casting his gaze down. "But I didn't want to risk it. With you gone, your grandmother no longer here to run the estate, and almost a dozen Blighted people living in the house, I didn't want to take the chance that Peacekeepers would show up and try to forcibly remove us."

"Holy shit," I breathed, gazing up at the enormous mansion. The cherry wood front door was framed by several tall, ornate white columns, and the pale facade of the mansion looked as pristine as ever.

What drew my attention, though, were the wards. Plural. As in, more than one.

Beatrice had kept a pretty strong ward over her house. The spell hadn't faded after her death, which meant she wasn't the caster—it was probably purchased from a security company. That had seemed like plenty of protection, even for a house as lavish as this one. But now, at least two new wards glittered over the one that had already been in place, making the whole building shimmer with a multicolored glow.

I ripped my gaze away from the glowing house and looked at Jae again. "You did all this?"

"Yes. If the Representatives decided to come after us, they could force whoever put her ward up to remove it, leaving us exposed. I simply made sure that can't happen… and added a few other protections while I was at it."

"No kidding," I murmured as we approached the front door. "This place is like a bunker."

The word immediately conjured visions of Rain's lair in the mountains, and I wished I'd chosen a different term. This wasn't a bunker, where a power-hungry madman spent his days plotting the downfall of civilization.

This was a haven.

"It was necessary, Lana." Jae's voice was soft. He held his palms out toward the door, and the wards parted to grant us entry. "The Representatives know you're harboring Blighted families here. They haven't let word of it get out yet, probably because it creates bad optics for them—one of their own being a Blighted sympathizer. But they could send Peacekeepers any time."

We entered the high-ceilinged foyer. Though this floor of the house was quiet, noises filtered down from upstairs.

Without asking this time, Fen swooped me up, one arm under my knees and the other under my shoulders. I wrapped my arms around his neck and rested my head on his chest, too worn out to protest. He carried me up to my room, and Akio opened the door for us before I was deposited on the king-sized bed.

Jae sat on the soft mattress beside me. Corin helped lift me up, and the two of them gently peeled off the single-sleeved shirt I'd taken from Kate. The remaining sleeve chafed against the bite wound on my shoulder, and I sucked in a sharp breath, pushing down the wave of nausea that passed through me.

At the sight of my injury, Jae's green eyes flashed, his normally calm expression hardening with anger. "You should've told me, Lana. I could've healed you on the mountain."

"There was no time." I shook my head, falling back against the pillows tiredly. "We made it back, didn't we?"

"We would have made it anyway! Godsdamn it, I knew you were hurt, but—"

He cut off and stood abruptly, pacing to the other side of the room, his back to me. I gazed after him in shock. I'd known he would be upset I didn't tell him about all my injuries, but I hadn't expected this strong of a reaction.

After a moment, Jae turned around. His face was composed again, but the green of his eyes still churned with agitation. He walked slowly to the bed and sat down, closer to me this time. He rested his strong, long-fingered hands on my bare stomach, and I clenched the muscles involuntarily as a shiver raced through me.

When he'd taught me to heal Corin, he told me to hover my hands over the injury, reaching out with my magic instead of with physical touch. Having Jae's hands on me, skin-to-skin as the bright glow of magic flowed from him into me, felt strangely intimate. His gaze traveled over me as he worked, roaming my body with a possessiveness and entitlement that made my heart beat faster.

The rest of my four stood sentry as he worked on me, but I couldn't tear my gaze away from Jae. The expression on his face was fierce, a mixture of anger and pain and... something else.

36

Something that made heat flare low in my belly, made my nipples harden and my skin ache for more of his touch.

His hand on my stomach moved up slightly, grazing the bottoms of my breasts, and my back nearly bowed off the bed. The combination of the healing magic pouring through my body and the feelings his touch elicited made me giddy. This was more than the absence of pain. This was ecstasy.

I closed my eyes and bit my lip, drawing in deep breaths through my nose as I got lost in the sensations coursing through me.

Sooner than I would've liked, Jae pulled his magic back and removed his hands, leaving my body free of pain but somehow still bereft. I blinked my eyes open to see him leaning over me, his face hovering above mine.

Time seemed to pause as I took in his elegant features. His long nose, high cheekbones, and slightly pointed chin, those clear green eyes that had always captivated me. He was gazing back at me with an equal intensity, and when he dipped his head toward mine, my heart fluttered.

But at the last moment, he changed course, pressing a kiss to my cheek instead of my lips. He lingered there for a second before drawing back, leaving only his ragged breaths echoing in my ears.

The other three men were gathered at the foot of the bed, watching us intently. Worry reflected in Corin's and Fen's eyes, but Akio looked at Jae with something like jealousy.

My brow furrowed. I didn't know what he had to be jealous about. Jae hadn't even kissed me on the lips. And if anyone had a right to get possessive, it was Corin or Fen. They'd made their feelings for me clear, while the incubus seemed to make a point of keeping me constantly guessing whether he actually liked me or not.

It took several heartbeats for me to shake off the almost trance-like state Jae had put me in, and I sat up slowly, letting my long red hair fall down over my shoulders. The ugly purple wound where the wolf had bit me was now little more than a light pink scar, although the blood and dirt smeared on my skin still remained. I touched my face tentatively but could feel nothing. No pain, no lump. It was completely healed.

I grinned at Jae, brushing past what had just transpired between us. "You're good."

His lips lifted in the calm smile I loved so much. "I've had a lot of practice."

My body was still a little weak—nothing but rest, food, and water would fix that—but I felt a million times better as I scooted toward the foot of the bed and stood up.

"I'm going to shower. I need to get the smell of that psychopath's dungeon off me. Then we need to talk."

"Yes." Jae's voice was grim, making me wonder what I'd missed in the days I'd been locked up. "We do."

THE FIRST TIME I'd stepped into the large stone-walled shower in my en suite bathroom at Beatrice's house, I'd thought it was the most luxurious feeling in the world.

I was wrong.

The most luxurious feeling in the world was stepping under the gentle spray of hot water after spending ten days locked in a dingy, cold, magic-suppressing cell.

Not that I ever planned on doing *that* again.

But the water cascading down my body, rinsing away all the dirt, grime, and blood, made me feel clean and new, possibly even up to all the challenges facing us. I let it pour over my face for a while longer once I was clean, emptying my mind for a few moments and just feeling.

As I pushed open the steamy glass door and stepped out, the weight of the world came crashing back down on me again. But the shower had revitalized me enough that my legs didn't buckle under the pressure.

My room was empty when I returned to it, the door to the hall shut. I threw on a soft, worn T-shirt and a pair of jeans and padded lightly down the stairs.

I poked my head into the darkened living room as I passed, but the television was off. Ivy was nowhere to be seen. *Huh.* Had she gone back to my old apartment in the Outskirts? Maybe she'd gotten bored here with me gone. Although I didn't see how that could be possible, as long as the TV still worked.

Voices drew me down the hall, and I smiled as I headed toward the kitchen, my four's usual meeting spot. Some things never changed.

I pushed the door open… and blinked.

Okay, maybe they changed a little.

My four were gathered around the large kitchen island, deep in conversation with Retta and Darcy. Retta's son William sat on the floor in the corner with his friend Sophie, playing cards quietly. And Ivy was perched on one of the counters, her wide brown eyes watching them all raptly.

Everyone looked up when I entered. William and Sophie gawped at me, and Retta and Darcy pushed away from the island to fuss over me.

"Oh, Miss Lana! We were so worried about you." Retta's soft

voice was more high-pitched than normal, and her eyes glistened behind her thick glasses.

"We've all been going near out of our minds trying to help your men find you," Darcy added, surprising me by pulling me into her large bosom for a hug. "They just told us it was Rain. I can't pretend to be surprised. I've heard awful things about that man. His Blighted house staff never last long."

I pulled back, eyebrows shooting up to my hairline. "You... you know?" I shot a glance at the men. "You told them?"

Retta and Darcy had gleaned a little bit of my history, but not much. And I certainly hadn't told them I was working against the government from the inside.

"They know everything, Lana," Corin informed me, his blue eyes warm and reassuring. "They took a blood oath; they'll keep our secrets."

My eyes bugged even wider. "They *what?*" I whipped my head back to the two women. "You *did?*"

"We wanted to, Miss Lana. We wanted to help, and we knew there was more going on than you'd told us. Jae explained there was no danger in the spell as long as we didn't intend on breaking our word. And we don't."

My mouth dropped open. Hearing Darcy talk so casually about having magic performed on her, and a powerful spell like a blood oath at that, was akin to hearing her mention offhandedly that Jae had dipped her hand in a vat of acid.

I scanned the room again, meeting the amused gazes of my four before looking back at Retta and Darcy. "*How* long was I gone?"

Fenris laughed out loud at that, and Darcy smiled indulgently before her expression sobered. "Long enough. Things have been moving fast."

"So I gather," I muttered, letting them usher me over to the island. "So, you know about the...?"

"Resistance?" Retta nodded, her wild mass of red-brown hair shifting with the movement. "Oh, yes. We've even met the new leader. We didn't know Christine, but this man... well, I for one believe in his vision."

Damn. Things really had moved fast. It made sense though. The Resistance was a large enough movement that it couldn't function without a leader for long. And with the escalation of violence against the Blighted and the Representatives' return to public executions, a strong rebel organization was needed more than ever.

"Who is he? What's he—?" I started to ask, but then cut myself off. "Wait. I need to hear about what's been going on, but first, I have to tell you what I learned. It changes everything."

Darcy settled me on the stool she'd vacated then went to the oven, pulling out a large dish that smelled like meat, cheese, and potatoes.

She served us all while I began to talk. I ate as fast as I could, speaking with my mouth full as I caught the guys up on what happened after Christine used the transport spell to pull me away. I knew I'd lose my appetite as soon as I got to the next part, and I needed the nourishment.

When I explained how Rain had manipulated Christine into working for him, Retta gasped, her eyes darting to William. My heart twinged. Using love to make people do awful things was just about the best definition of evil I could think of.

I went on to tell them how Kate had killed Christine, and that I'd then attempted to kill Rain. When I reached the part where he admitted he was responsible for the Great Death, my lips kept moving, my voice reporting the facts clearly and evenly. But my mind rebelled as it always did when I tried to fully comprehend what Rain had done.

There wasn't a punishment to fit that crime. There were barely adequate words to describe it.

By the time I finished talking, everyone's forks were down, food left half-eaten on their plates. *Shit.* I should've warned them this wasn't a good dinnertime conversation.

Silence hung heavy in the air, but I didn't try to break it. I'd had days to process this revelation, and I still felt nauseated just thinking about it.

Finally, Corin spoke, his voice harsh and halting. "He let everyone think... *we* had done it."

His nostrils flared, and a muscle in his jaw flexed rhythmically. I reached across the island and grabbed his hand, squeezing it tightly. I knew he was thinking about his family. Rain had caused two great tragedies in his reckless pursuit of power, and everyone in this room had been affected by them somehow.

Well, except maybe Ivy.

But when I glanced over at the ghost, her translucent brown eyes glistened with tears, and her delicate chin quivered.

I guess even the dead can see how fucked up this is.

"We have to tell the Representatives," Jae said. "It won't undo what's done. But they have to know."

"Will they listen?" Akio raised an eyebrow. His voice was smooth, but his complexion was slightly paler than usual.

"We'll make them." Jae pushed his plate away. "They'll have to—"

He was interrupted as the kitchen door swung open. A middle-aged man with a shiny scalp and tufts of brown hair on the sides of his head walked in, followed by two young teens. The boy froze midstride, and the girl let out a squeak as her gaze fell on me. The older man hesitated too, looking at me with an almost awed expression. Then he turned and hustled the kids out of the kitchen.

I frowned. "What was that about? They're not scared of me because I'm Gifted, are they? Didn't you tell them I don't care about that?"

Darcy nodded, not meeting my eyes as she busied herself with clearing away plates. "Oh, yes, we told them."

Twisting my still-damp hair around my fist, I looked back toward the door. "Then what—?"

"They probably just can't believe it's you," Ivy interjected, her voice returning to its usual brightness as she wiped away the tears on her cheeks. "It's one thing to see you on a building or on TV. It's another thing to see The Crow in person."

I shook my head in confusion. "The… *what?*"

"That's one of the things we have to tell you about," Fen muttered, poking at invisible crumbs on the kitchen island. Now nobody seemed willing to meet my eyes.

"What? Tell me about what?"

"Oh, I'll show you!" Ivy hopped off the counter, gesturing for me to follow before walking through the kitchen door.

Dear gods. What now?

CHAPTER 6

My STOMACH FELT like a lump of cement as I strode down the hall behind Ivy.

I was seriously regretting having eaten at all, especially so fast. Darcy's delicious food was sure to taste much worse on the way back up, and that was exactly where it wanted to go.

The men trailed after me, and when I entered the living room and stood behind the couch, they gathered close by. They might not think I was going to be happy about whatever Ivy was going to show me, but they were still here to support me. I reached out and grabbed two hands, feeling two others fall on my shoulders.

Ivy settled onto the couch then reached for the remote on the coffee table, a look of extreme concentration on her face. She slowly brought her finger down, and the TV flickered on, sound blazing. She brought it down again, and the volume muted.

Her head whipped toward me, pride shining on her face. I would've teasingly congratulated her for pressing the buttons herself, but the image that popped up on the screen arrested that thought.

It was me.

But... not.

It was a stenciled image of me, looking up and slightly away from the viewer. The image was created in blocks of color, but my features were unmistakable. Above my head, there was a stencil of a crow in flight, wings spread wide.

"Fuck," I whispered. It was the only word I could think of at the moment.

The camera panned out, and I realized it had been zoomed in tight on the side of a tall building in the Capital. I'd been near there once before in pursuit of a mark. The building was downtown, and it was usually covered in pictures of Secretary General Theron Stearns.

As the camera continued to pull away, my breath caught. Posters of my face with the crow above it were pasted over and over again along the facade of the building. And in the middle, a twenty-foot tall mural was painted in full color.

Me again.

In a flowing blue dress the color of the ocean.

And flanking me were each of my four, their formation creating a V with me at the tip.

"What is this?" My words were soft but had a panicked edge to them, and I squeezed Fenris's and Jae's hands so hard their bones grated. "What the hell is this?"

"This was Noble's idea," Jae answered softly, not attempting to extract his hand from my bruising grip.

"Who the fuck is Noble?" I spun wildly around to face the men. "What's going on?"

"He's the new leader of the Resistance. He stepped in to take Christine's place," Corin said. "He's a good man, Lana."

"'Good?' Isn't that what you said about Christine?" I shot

back, then immediately regretted it. Christine's betrayal had rocked them too, and she'd hurt us all with her actions. It wasn't fair of me to blame them for her treachery. Or to blame this Noble guy, whoever he was.

Corin's gaze lowered. "It is. And we were wrong. But we have to trust someone, Lana. Or the Resistance will fall apart."

"When we told everyone Christine betrayed us, infighting immediately broke out." Fen ran a hand through his dark hair. "Some people believed us, and some didn't. It was getting ugly. But Noble stepped up. He helped us convince the doubters and brought everyone back together. He's young, but he's bold. Wait 'til you meet him to judge him."

I slumped against the back of the couch. "Okay. Fine. But that doesn't explain *this*." I gestured to the screen behind me. "What am I doing on the side of a building?"

"It's a good likeness of you, isn't it?" Ivy turned around on the sofa to join our conversation. Her nose wrinkled as she peered at me. "Although I've only ever seen you wear a dress once. They should've painted you in black."

"Why did they paint me at all?"

"Noble wants to move faster. Christine was cautious, limiting our activities to disrupting shipping lines and bringing what aid we could to Blighted people, but Noble thinks—and I agree with him—that the time to hold back is over." Corin lifted his gaze to mine again, determination blazing in his blue irises. "We're looking at a return to the worst period after the Great Death, when no Blighted person was safe. People in the Outskirts know it. They're afraid, and they're angry."

"They need a symbol." Akio's voice was smooth. "That's you, kitten."

I blinked. "A symbol of what?"

"Of hope." His dark eyes glittered, their depths drawing me in like a magnetic force. "Of what the world could be."

"How?"

"You're a Blighted woman, suddenly turned Gifted. But you haven't left your people behind. You're still one of them. And you will fight for them."

"I…." My voice trailed off.

I couldn't deny I still subconsciously included myself among the Blighted and probably always would. And it was true I'd come to the Capital with the sole intention of aiding the Resistance. But it was one thing to think and do those things secretly, in private. It was another thing altogether to be made into some sort of symbol, some larger-than-life icon of an entire movement.

Fuck. I couldn't even fill out Kate's shoes. There was no way I could fit into the shoes of that twenty-foot-tall version of myself.

"The Resistance has stopped hiding, killer." Fen bounced on the balls of his feet, his excitement palpable. "We've come out of the shadows. We're openly recruiting—and people are coming to us in droves. The headquarters are filled to capacity, but sub-cells have been forming all around the Outskirts. It keeps the Representatives on their toes, and keeps us light on our feet."

My head spun, trying to process everything. "So… the Representatives know I'm with the Resistance?" I glanced at Jae. "No wonder you warded the shit out of this place."

He shook his head. "No, the Resistance has never claimed you as a member. I'm sure the Representatives suspect, but all Noble has done is take what was already public knowledge about you and shape it into a compelling story." Warmth flashed in his emerald eyes. "It didn't take much. Your story *is* incredible, Lana."

"So now I'm just 'The Crow?' What does that mean? What do I do?"

"You don't *do* anything, kitten. Or rather, you just do what comes naturally and let the legend take care of itself." Akio's voice held an amused tone that made me want to punch him.

Scrubbing my hands over my face, I let out a growl. "Right. Let the legend take care of itself. I *really* can't wait to meet this Noble guy."

"He's eager to meet you too," Jae said. Then his face darkened. "But we have to prioritize stopping Rain. If he succeeds in another magic pull, the Resistance's entire goal will be moot. Whether it kills the Gifted this time or merely strips their magic, the end result either way will be widespread chaos and death. The fewer hands power is concentrated in, the harder it becomes to wrest back control."

The dinner I'd just eaten turned into a rock in my stomach. "Rain told me he needed the magic from just a few more strong mages to power the spell, and he got to at least one man before me. But as far as I know, I was the only prisoner left in his compound. So my escape should slow him down at least a little bit. Shit. I should've tried to find his machine and break it while I was there."

"No, you shouldn't have," Jae said sternly. "You were weak and badly injured, and I'm sure it's well protected. We need more magical firepower on our side before we attempt to destroy it."

"Or we could just kill Rain." My words sounded bloodthirsty, but I didn't care. I was sick of death following me around, but I'd make an exception for that fucker.

"We can't. Not yet." Corin's voice was strained, as if it pained him to say it.

48

I whipped my head toward him. "Why the fuck not? He's a murdering psychopath!"

"We know, killer. But it's bigger than just him. He's our proof that the Blighted didn't cause the Great Death." Fenris ducked his head to catch my eyes. "If he dies before the truth gets out, his secret will die with him."

"They're right," Jae said softly. "We need to let the world know what he's done. We need to let the Representatives know."

I threw a glance over my shoulder at the television.

The screen was now displaying a witch and warlock squaring off over two cauldrons in some kind of brewing contest, but all I could see was the image of myself, larger-than-life in a sweeping blue dress. My four behind me. The silhouette of a crow above my head.

Those were some awfully damn big shoes to fill.

But I had to try.

I turned back to face the men, forcing my unwilling body to press away from the couch and stand straight. "Then tomorrow, I guess I better crash another council meeting."

THERE WAS a time in my life when, regardless of the wisdom of my decision, I would've marched right back up the mountainside to Rain's lair in the middle of the night and thrown myself headfirst into a battle I was ill-prepared for and likely to lose—just because I couldn't stand waiting.

As I stared up at the dark ceiling in my bedroom, I sort of wished I was still that person.

Fuck waiting.

Fuck strategizing and playing angles and luring people into traps.

There was a bad man out there planning to do very bad things, and if I died trying to stop him... well, that was better than not trying, right?

But I couldn't think like that anymore. When I was just a loner mercenary living and working on my own, I could be as rash and impulsive as I liked. If I made a mistake or didn't think things through, the only one to suffer for it would be me. But now, there were four men who needed me to stay alive. Hundreds of Resistance members who believed I was some sort of leader. And thousands of others whose lives depended on me, whether they knew it or not. If I acted impulsively, I wasn't just gambling with my own life; I was risking all of theirs.

That thought was *not* helping me sleep.

My four were curled up on the large bed with me, each one of them touching me in some way. Jae's hand grasped mine, our fingers interlaced. Fen was spooning Jae to get closer to me, his large palm resting on my stomach. Corin was curled up on my other side, and Akio's hand was tangled in my hair. The patterns of our breath played off each other, forming a singular sound—as if we were one entity.

It felt like that sometimes. Like we were parts of a whole, each of us strong in our own right, but unstoppable together.

Gods, I hoped that was true.

Not wanting to disturb anyone, but too jittery to keep staring at the ceiling in silence, I released Jae's hand and slid downward then crawled off the foot of the bed. When I turned to look back, a smile parted my lips despite my churning anxiety. The men had all shifted slightly, closing up the gap I'd left behind. But I knew as soon as I returned, the space would open back up for me.

I crept downstairs, through the quiet house, and out the back door. Jae had keyed me into the new wards, but I still glanced up at the glow around the house warily as I entered the sprawling garden.

The moon was high in the sky, casting a bright blue light over the flowers and hedges that lined the path. There was a chill in the air, and I wrapped my arms around myself. It wasn't unbearable, but after ten days of being too cold all the time, my body craved warmth.

When I reached the bench we'd gathered around the day my four first arrived here, I sat down, pulling my knees up to my chest. I closed my eyes and inhaled the sweet scent of lilacs.

I wish Beatrice were here. I wish I could talk to her.

Twice, Rain had taken us from each other.

I couldn't get her back, but I'd be damned if I let him destroy any other families.

"Couldn't sleep?"

The voice made me jump, and my eyes flew open as I instinctively summoned a small flame.

Akio held his hands out. "Relax, kitten. No need to greet me with your usual level of violence."

I snorted but snuffed the flame. "No, I couldn't sleep. Sorry, I tried not to wake anyone when I left."

"You didn't. I was already awake." His eyes were like reflections of the night sky above, glimmering with starlight.

The incubus sank languidly onto the bench beside me, and we sat in silence for a few moments. When I rubbed the goose bumps on my arms, he glanced over at me. Then he leaned forward, pulling his dark, long-sleeved Henley over his head.

He held it out to me, and I quirked an eyebrow. "You really will use any excuse to take your shirt off, won't you?"

"I could let you die of hypothermia if you prefer," he said dryly, making me purse my lips to hide a smile. Gods, he really was dramatic.

"All right, give me that."

I swiped the large shirt from his hands and slipped it on over my tank top, relishing the way his warmth and scent still clung to it. I almost lifted it to my nose to inhale the spicy smell of him, but caught myself—though maybe not fast enough, if his smug grin was any indication.

"So, what keeps a kitten awake at night when she should be resting and recovering?"

I huffed a laugh and gave him a sideways glance. "Seriously?"

"What? I'm not allowed to ask?"

"No, you are. It's just... you really want to know?"

"Why not?" One side of his mouth lifted, and I couldn't help but remember how soft his lips had felt against mine. "I can be a good listener. If it helps, pretend I'm Jae."

I sputtered, his words catching me off guard. What did he mean by that? "I don't only confide in him! I talk to Corin and Fen all the time. And I'll talk to you anytime if you just ask."

"I thought that's what I just did."

Oh. He had me there.

Feeling suddenly awkward, I rubbed my hands on my soft pants. "Well, I think an easier question to answer would be what's *not* keeping me up. There's so much, Akio. So much to do, so much to consider. So much riding on this. I'm not used to taking care of anyone but myself, and I don't feel qualified for any of the responsibility I've been given." I paused, giving him a chance to jump in and say something comforting, but he just watched me, his tattooed arms crossed over his chest. So I went on. "I don't know who to trust anymore. Besides you four, I mean. There

52

have been so many lies, so much betrayal. Corin says we have to trust someone to move forward, but I'm so scared of being wrong again."

I ran out of words then, though thoughts continued to streak like comets through my mind.

Akio shifted his gaze to the small burbling fountain nestled among the flowers in the garden, his tongue darting out to wet his lips.

"I loved a woman once."

My eyes went wide. That was not at all what I'd expected him to say. I angled my body toward his a little, trying not to make my intense interest too obvious. "Oh?"

He smiled sardonically. "Don't sound so surprised, kitten. I *am* capable of the emotion."

"Uh, right. I mean, of course."

"This was many, many years ago. Long before the Great Death, before the Resistance. When I was just a human trying to find my way in the world. Looking for someone to build a life with." He sighed softly. "Then I found Ria. She was beautiful, intelligent, and sophisticated. A powerful mage. Too good for me, I was sure. But she wanted me, and I didn't question my good fortune. Our affair was like a whirlwind; even now, looking back on it, it almost doesn't seem real. Days and nights spent in each other's arms, the entire world forgotten."

I picked at a thread on my pants, trying to unwind the knot of jealousy hardening in my stomach. "Sounds… nice."

"Oh, kitten." He chuckled. "It was more than nice. It was sin made corporeal. It was pleasure unlike any I had ever experienced." Akio shifted next to me, his body growing tense. His voice dropped. "She evidently felt the same way. But while I was convinced I'd fallen in love with her, despite having known her just a few short weeks, she wanted me for nothing more than sex."

"Oh...." I said dumbly, my gut twisting for an entirely different reason now.

"While I was making plans to ask her to marry me, she made a deal with a god and cast a powerful spell to turn me into an incubus. Apparently, it wasn't enough for us to share our bodies willingly, out of love. She wanted to own the pleasure I gave her, to preserve it and control it. She turned me into a demon of lust to serve her."

Holy fuck.

Silence settled between us, broken only by the call of an owl in the distance.

My heart ached at the pain in Akio's smooth voice. Though he might claim the memory was so old it felt like a dream, the wound was real, and it was still fresh. I didn't know why he was telling me this right now, but I got the feeling he hadn't shared the story with many people.

And shit, no wonder he was always so hot and cold with me, why he seemed to chafe at the connection my magic wove between us more than the others did. I'd rebelled against the bond myself for a long time, because it brought back terrifying echoes of my indentured servitude to the Gifted man, Edgar. I hadn't been able to see a "bond" as anything positive, only as a loss of control and subjugation to another person. Given Akio's history, I was sure he felt the same.

"I'm sorry. That's awful. What did you do?" I nudged him gently.

He looked down at me, the angles of his beautiful face hard in the moonlight.

"I did just what she intended. I served her pleasure for many years. She had turned me into a creature of lust, and I had no control over my instincts at first. But gradually, I began to come back to myself, flashes of the man I had been in life returning. And when I was fully in control once again, I killed her."

My breath hitched.

I wasn't surprised to hear that, nor particularly sorry he'd done it. That fucking bitch deserved what she got.

But I wished he hadn't had to. I wished he'd found someone who cared about him enough to want love from him as well as sex—even if that meant his life took a different path and I never got to meet him.

"I'm so sorry, Akio. You deserved better than that." The words were paltry, but they were all I had to offer.

He stared at me for a long moment, his eyes inscrutable in the darkness, before he spoke again.

"Don't trust anyone more than they give you reason to, kitten."

And with that, he stood and walked back toward the house, his tattoos shifting under the moonlight, his gait oddly stiff.

CHAPTER 7

"What happened to Tarik?"

I glanced at the back of the unfamiliar fairy's head as he drove us to the palace. His deep blue, almost purple hair was a stark contrast to the bright green locks of Beatrice's usual driver.

"He... left." Fen grimaced.

His tone made me curious. "What does that mean?"

"Well, he quit. And we're pretty sure he's the one who told the Representatives that you're sheltering Blighted families in your grandmother's house."

My eyebrows shot up. "What? But he's the one who went to pick them up!"

"Yeah. Because you told him to. And his job was to serve Beatrice—and you. But he wasn't exactly happy about bringing the Blighted into the Capital. After you disappeared, so did he."

Leaning back against the seat, I stared out at the large estates we drove past. "Well, shit."

Sometimes I forgot the enormity of what faced us. There were the looming, obvious threats—Rain's magic pull, mass violence against the Blighted. But then there were the smaller, more pervasive and mundane obstacles. Like the fact that even a genuinely nice guy like the green-haired fairy, Tarik, held such a deep-rooted prejudice against the Blighted that he couldn't abide by my decision to invite them into my grandmother's home.

"But Elren is great!" Fenris tapped the back of the driver's seat enthusiastically, and fairy magic flooded the car, making joy bubble up within me. "He helped us search for you. Called in some connections."

I was tempted to ask if Elren knew about the Resistance and had taken a blood oath too, but zipped my mouth shut. My guess was that the fairy had been kept on a need-to-know basis, only told that I was missing, but not given more details about why. Although the Resistance could use more magical support, it was harder to convince the Gifted, or even the Touched, to turn against a government that had favored them for so long.

"It was my pleasure, sir. I'm glad you're found, Miss Crow." The fairy glanced at me through the rearview mirror, his eyes the same deep blue as his hair. I smiled at him and dipped my head, not missing the fact that he called me "Crow" instead of "Lockwood." He must've seen the propaganda Noble was spreading. Maybe he was more sympathetic to our cause than I'd thought.

Before I had time to consider that further, we pulled to a stop outside the palace. Guards lined the steps like they had in the days after Beatrice was killed. Apparently, security was still elevated.

We stepped out of the large SUV and Elren pulled away. All of my four had insisted on coming to the palace with me this morning to confront Rain; Corin had looked ready to fight anyone who tried to make him stay behind. I hadn't argued.

There was strength in numbers, and after ten days apart, I needed them near me.

It felt a little strange to try to recruit help from the Representatives at the same time we were attempting to undermine them. But Jae was right. We needed more magical firepower to stop Rain. Then we'd deal with the rest of the Gifted government.

The guards watched us walk quickly up the steps, but no one moved to stop us. I wondered how much longer I could skate by on my grandmother's legacy and my family name. Probably not long, if Noble kept wallpapering the city with images of me as an icon of rebellion. Even if the Resistance didn't claim me as one of their own, the Representatives couldn't be happy about the granddaughter of one of their esteemed members being associated with a rebel group.

We walked in a tight cluster, drawing curious stares and some outright glares from palace staff as we headed up to the fifth floor. At least by now I knew my way around well enough not to have to stop and ask a guard for directions.

When we reached the large double doors to the council room, I hesitated. Would Rain be in there? Or was he busy dealing with the fallout from my escape? Finding a new Gifted person to pull magic from?

A hand fell on the small of my back, and I looked over into Jae's serious face.

"You can do this, Lana. We're all behind you."

I shot him a grateful smile then pushed the doors open, leading the way into the room. It probably broke all kinds of palace protocol for me to bring my four men into a council meeting. I'd also forgone the fancy dresses for a more practical outfit of dark jeans and a long-sleeved top, but we were about to throw a metaphorical pipe bomb into the place anyway. Hopefully, once the Representatives heard what I had to say, my outfit and the company I brought with me would be the least of their concerns.

Just as they had the first time I'd shown up at a meeting, everyone in the room froze to look up at me.

Theron sat at the head of the table like always. In fact, everyone seemed to be in the same seats they'd occupied last time.

Including Rain.

The Chief Advisor sat at Theron's left side, and he straightened in his chair at the sight of me, his eyes widening. Although he was a good actor, he couldn't hide the brief flash of shock and fear on his face. Had he hoped I'd died on the mountain trying to escape? Had he thought I wouldn't come here?

"Hey, Rain," I said casually, coming to stand at the opposite end of the long table from Theron. "Surprised to see me?"

"Miss Lockwood." His raspy voice was blandly pleasant. "I'm... relieved to see you."

"What the hell is this? Is she allowed to parade her pets all over the palace now?" Nicholas shot out of his seat, jumping straight past the surprise at my sudden reappearance to his anger at the presence of my four.

I saw Jae and Akio step in front of Corin, and although I knew he must be chafing at the protection, I was glad for it. Not one of us doubted Corin's abilities, but as a team, we looked out for each other.

"Miss Lockwood." Theron raised his hand, not so much in a greeting as to quiet the room. He looked older than he had last time I'd seen him, his face more tired. "What is the meaning of this? I allowed you a place on this council because of the many years of dedicated service your grandmother gave us. But you've taken the good faith I put in you and twisted it beyond recognition. You clearly have no place in this government or in this palace."

"Blighted-lover!" Nicholas spat, baring his teeth. His gaunt face was pulled into a threatening scowl. No one else at the large table looked much friendlier.

Victor Kruger rose slowly to his feet, and tension crackled through the room.

"I'm not here to try to reclaim Beatrice's council seat," I said, my voice rising with each word. I needed to get this out fast before things got ugly. "I'm here because I have information that concerns all Gifted."

At that, Rain surged to his feet. "If you're not a member of this council, you have no right to be here, Miss Lockwood. Leave, now."

I tilted my head at him. "Aw, Rain. What about the *obligation* you have to my family? What about your promise to help me?"

"What promise?" Jonas Nocturne looked past Theron to Rain, who shifted uncomfortably.

"Oh, you didn't hear about that? Didn't you know he promised to help me root out who killed my grandmother? He could've made my search much easier by just admitting *he* did it."

Rain scoffed as several sets of eyes turned to him. "You've gone quite mad, Miss Lockwood."

I slammed my hands down on the table and leaned toward him. "Yeah, I am mad. I'm fucking furious. You lied to us all, Rain. Me and everyone in this room. You killed Beatrice. You've been the one abducting Gifted citizens from the Capital. *You* created the spell that caused the Great Death."

The room went quiet, and now everyone was looking at Rain.

My heart thundered in my chest, but I didn't move, keeping my gaze pinned on him.

His mouth opened slowly, as if he were considering his next words carefully. When he spoke, his voice was soft. "*This* was your plan, Miss Lockwood? March into a council meeting and accuse me of something so ludicrous, so outrageous?" He chuckled lightly, the wrinkles at the corners of his eyes deepening. "How exactly did you think that would work?"

I clenched my jaw, my hands fisting on the table. I couldn't tell if he was acting or addressing me honestly right now. Maybe a little bit of both.

"It's true! He tried to pull magic from people, but it fucking killed them. And he's planning to do it again. He's got a bunker up in the mountains that he—"

Rain's laugh interrupted me. "Listen to yourself, Miss Lockwood! You sound insane. Why would anyone on this council believe you when, as our esteemed Secretary General just pointed out, you've made your allegiances perfectly clear? The man behind you, Akio Sun, is a known Resistance member."

"*What?*" Simon Gaunt's head snapped in our direction, his too-smooth face aghast. I remembered how upset he'd been about the Gifted abductions and the attacks on the palace. He seemed to operate entirely from a place of fear.

"Known, huh?" I ground out. Jae's magic swelled behind me, and I could tell he was preparing to fight our way out of here if we had to. But I wasn't done trying to show the Representatives what was right under their noses. "Known to you, because *you* were put in charge of gathering intel on the Resistance—of hiring mercenaries to take out targets that might be a threat to the government. But you didn't stop there, did you? No, you hired those same mercenaries to bring you Gifted and Touched lab rats for you to experiment on."

Rain stood tall, somehow managing to look imperiously down his nose at me from several yards away. "This has gone on long enough. Secretary General, I cannot allow her to continue spreading such unconscionable lies about me." He glanced across the table to where Victor and Nicholas sat side by side, practically salivating like junkyard dogs hungry for a fight. "Perhaps you were right. We have given the Blighted too much freedom. It's time to put them back in their place."

The two men grinned viciously, and Eben Knowles shifted away from them, as though the bloodlust emanating from them made him uncomfortable.

"He's talking about you, you know!" I wanted to grab every person at this table and shake them, force them to see how their own prejudices were feeding right into Rain's hands. "Once he performs another magic pull, *you'll* be fucking Blighted. And whatever magic users are left will grind you into the dirt like you're less than nothing." I pointed a shaky finger at Rain. "He'll make sure of that."

"What evidence do you have, Miss Lockwood?" Olene asked. Her striking double-hued blue eyes were narrowed, making the dark rims around her irises look almost black. But my heart leapt at her words. If she was asking, that must mean she hadn't decided outright that I was lying.

"I have nothing with me. But he told me himself. And I know where his compound is. He built some kind of a machine powered by magic—it's in the mountains, where he kept me locked up for the past ten days."

"Lies." Rain's raspy voice was louder now, a little less controlled than when we'd walked in. Was he getting nervous?

His magic pulsed from him like a heartbeat, feeling stronger than I remembered. "Lies told by a woman who, whatever magic she may possess, will always be Blighted at heart."

"At least I *have* a fucking heart, you asshole!"

"Minister of Justice, remove her." Theron's voice was hard, his wrinkles deepened by the scowl on his face. "And arrest the Resistance member. Arrest all of them."

I straightened, taking two steps back to stand protectively in front of my four. Pivoting, I faced Olene. She was my only hope now. "Why don't you just look? I can take you there. I can show you."

"Where is it?" Olene rose slowly, her gaze fixed on me.

"In the Rocky Mountains, ten miles south of—"

"Jonas!" Rain bellowed, sweeping his arm toward me. Jae's father leapt to his feet, his magic flaring.

Damn it. We were out of time.

CHAPTER 8

JAE STEPPED QUICKLY to my side, throwing his hands out. A shimmering veil of white burst from his fingertips, settling into a wide barrier between the Representatives and us. It spanned the entire room, floor to ceiling and wall to wall. Nicholas and Victor had joined Jonas as he approached, but they paused at the sight of the barrier, scowling.

"What...?" I glanced at him.

"Shield. It's strong, but it won't hold them for long. And it won't stop—"

Before he could finish speaking, the doors behind us burst open, and a dozen Touched guards in white-and-blue uniforms streamed in. Jonas must've summoned them. Light flared around two of the men. They shifted into panthers, dropping low onto their haunches as they prepared to pounce.

A warlock at the front of the group pulled the stopper on a small vial and flung the contents toward us. The droplets turned to mist as they neared me, and as the mist enveloped me, my body seemed to slow. It felt like I was moving underwater, or on a two-second time delay. I raised my hands to throw a fireball at the warlock and watched in dismay as my arms moved sluggishly upward.

He wasn't hampered by the time slow-down like I was, and his movements seemed incredibly fast as he hurled another potion at me. Someone yanked me out of the way, and my brain felt like it hovered in empty space outside my body for several beats. Fen's arms wrapped around me from behind, his breath hot on my ear. "You okay, killer?"

"Y...esss...." The word stretched out of my mouth like taffy, and before I was even finished speaking, he'd whirled us around. Blue fireballs flew past my head as Jae traded blows with a water elementalist. The white barrier he'd erected in the middle of the room was losing strength, becoming more and more translucent as the Representatives and guards battered it with spells.

Akio looked like he'd been hit by the same potion as me. Corin had an arm around his waist and was hauling him toward the door. It opened, revealing more guards on the other side. My heart thudded heavily in my chest, the beat too slow for the panic coursing through my veins.

"C...orin...!" I drew my hand up, fighting against the sluggish feeling of the spell so hard my muscles ached.

His head whipped around, and he delivered a punishing kick to the midsection of the first guard, a demon with blue skin. The first guard flew backward into the one behind him, and they both toppled over.

Fenris dragged me toward Corin and Akio, and Jae followed close behind us. My body still felt like it was filled with sand, but I reached inside for my magic, summoning wind this time. Not even lifting my hands to guide it, I just let it swirl around us, faster and faster, creating a small tornado with the five of us at the center.

The shield Jae had put up broke, and lightning flashed toward us from Nicholas's fingertips. It got caught in the whirling wind around us, electrifying the air and making my hair stand on end.

"Tr...ansport spell!" I screamed, reaching for the one I had tucked away. My movements were too fucking slow, but Fen dug his hand roughly into my pocket, grabbing the small glass cylinder.

"Everyone hold on!" he shouted.

I felt a hand clamp onto my shoulder as he dropped the vial at our feet. Before it could roll away, he brought his booted foot down hard, shattering it.

Purple smoke rose up around us. Through the haze, I caught a glimpse of Jonas's angry face and Rain's triumphant one. Then my vision was obscured completely.

When the smoke cleared, bright sunshine poured down on us. We were in a field of tall grass, interrupted by a few tall cottonwoods. In the far distance, a line of dilapidated houses crouched like beasts on the horizon.

Fen released me, and I staggered forward, pitching from side to side as the world seemed to tilt underneath me. My limbs still weren't functioning quite right. I turned around, scanning our group to make sure we had everyone—and that we hadn't brought along any unwanted guests.

Akio swayed on his feet much like I did. Corin kept a hand on him to stop him from tipping over. Fen had a cut over his eye and was panting like a hot wolf. Jae looked calm, as usual, but even he was out of breath.

"Is everyone… all right?" I forced the words out, willing my mouth to cooperate.

"Yeah, we'll live." Fen wiped a sleeve across his forehead, clearing the blood. It was a small enough cut that blood didn't keep pouring from the wound.

"Gr…eat. Where… are we?" I squinted at our surroundings again.

"The Outskirts," Jae answered. "Near one of the portals to the Resistance base. But not too near. I didn't want to risk leading the guards directly there if any of them managed to slip into our transport spell."

He reached for Fen's forehead, but the shifter batted his hand away, muttering something about not needing every little cut healed like Akio did. Akio overheard him and tried to fix an affronted look on his face, but his muscles wouldn't cooperate.

This weird time-delay spell was starting to make me nauseated. It was like my entire body was an echo.

"Let's go then." I spoke clearly and slowly, and was pleased that the words came out a little easier this time.

Jae led us all through the field, toward one of the abandoned houses on the horizon. Fen hovered close by, but let me forge ahead on my own. My movements grew progressively less jerky, and by the time we reached the house, I was able to put one foot smoothly in front of the other again. Thank fuck for that. I still felt a little queasy, but now that I could walk in a straight line, the nausea was easier to ignore.

"We should've come here first." As my brain and body synced up again, bitter regret lanced through me. "What a fucking waste of time that was. I should've known those assholes wouldn't believe me. Not even to save their own skins."

"It wasn't a total waste." Jae pushed open the door, which sagged on its hinges, and ushered us inside. "Olene believed you."

I batted at a cobweb as we passed through the dark living room then wiped my hand off on the dusty couch. "No, she didn't. She wanted to. Or she was at least willing to consider it, if I'd had hard evidence to give her. But what was I supposed to do? Bring that massive fucking ball of magic down the mountain with me? Take Kate hostage? And why would they take her word if they wouldn't believe mine?"

"They wouldn't," Corin said grimly. We walked single-file up a set of rickety stairs and into a bedroom on the second floor.

"It's exactly like Beatrice said," I muttered. "My presence —*your* presence—challenges everything they want to believe. And so does suggesting the Great Death was caused by one man, and a Gifted man at that. If it's true, then they don't have a reason to punish and subjugate the Blighted anymore. They'd have to admit they did it with no cause in the first place. Are they really so desperate to cling to the way things are now that they'll ignore the truth?"

"Yes." Jae's voice was soft but blunt.

"But if Rain does another magic pull, where will that leave them? If they turn Blighted, their actions now will only have made things worse for themselves."

We stopped in front a pulsing blue portal inside the empty bedroom closet, and Jae shot me a glance, his green eyes sad.

"True. But I'm sure some would take that risk even if they did believe you. The fewer people who have magic, the more powerful those few will be; some of the Gifted would likely take that gamble, would risk losing everything on the chance of gaining even more."

I gaped at him. "That's fucking sick."

"No argument."

He walked through the portal, and the rest of us followed quickly after. The musty, dingy passage we stepped into no longer caught me by surprise. This was the network of tunnels underneath the abandoned factory where the Resistance was based. I hadn't been here for several weeks, but it looked—and smelled—exactly the same.

Jae sent up a ball of light and led the way through the tunnels to the guardroom. Inside the room, two burly men and two women stood sentry by the entrance to the Resistance compound, all heavily armed.

I was used to being greeted with suspicion or open hostility by the Blighted Resistance members, so I was shocked as hell when their gazes fell on me and they dipped their heads in a sign of respect. One of the women peeked up, her wide brown eyes darting from me to the men flanking me.

"We're here to see Noble. He's requested a meeting with Lana." Corin stepped forward, taking the lead as he usually did when dealing with the Blighted.

"The Crow?" One of the men peered around Corin to stare at me again. "I heard you saved a bunch of Blighted folk whose apartment complex got burned down. And you were the one who outed Christine as a traitor!"

I hesitated, taken aback. "Um…."

"Yes," Akio said smoothly, stepping up to my side. "That was her."

"I knew it. I recognized that red hair!" The man stepped aside, gesturing to his fellow guards to do the same.

Their gazes burned into me as we passed through the door, and as soon as it thudded closed behind us, I rounded on Akio. "Look, I don't know what Noble's plan is, but I don't like having lies told about me. Did you charm them into believing you?"

"Oh, kitten. If I used charm, you'd know it." His voice was teasing, but his expression darkened slightly.

Before I could identify the emotion on his face, Corin spoke. "He wasn't lying, Lana. Those people living at Beatrice's house? A gifted mob torched their building. You may not have been there when it happened, but you did save them."

I blinked, unsure how to respond to that. I hadn't even known. I'd just given them a place to stay, in rooms that weren't even being used. That didn't make me a fucking hero.

"Yeah, well, I don't like 'embellishing the truth' any more than I like lying," I said finally, as we made our way through the large compound. It was packed with people, at least twice as many as there had been last time I was here. "Tell Noble I'm either inspiring enough as I am, or I'm not. He doesn't get to make shit up about me to fit whatever storyline he's creating."

"I dunno. I think you're plenty inspiring, killer. Anyway, you can tell him yourself."

Fenris led the way onto the old factory floor. The abandoned machines and conveyor belts glinted in the shafts of light that cut through high, boarded-up windows. Against one wall, a metal staircase led up to an enclosed area on the second floor that had been the foreman's office.

The walls had once been floor-to-ceiling glass, though all but one panel was broken now. Sheets had been tacked over the other panels last time I was here, but they were down now, leaving the space more open and bright. I wondered if the new leader still called it the "war room" like Christine had.

Several people sat at the large table inside the open room. They all looked up as the metal staircase clanged under our footsteps, and I could guess immediately which one was Noble. I also began to understand how so much had changed in the short time since Christine had abducted me.

The group stood as we entered, and most of the men and women excused themselves, stepping past us on their way out. Only three remained. The man in the middle was about my height, with dark skin and close-cropped hair. He was wiry but well built, and I had no doubt that every one of his lean muscles served a purpose. His high cheekbones and pointed chin contrasted with his broad nose, and his dark eyes gleamed with intelligence.

But more noticeable than any of that was the energy that radiated from him. He was Blighted, so it wasn't magical power; it was just… him. This was not the kind of man who took things slow or did things by halves. This was a man who built a legend out of a scrappy ex-mercenary in less than two weeks.

The other two Resistance members, a man and woman, stepped back silently as Noble came around the table toward us. Every movement he made seemed spring-loaded.

"You must be The Crow." He smiled at me.

"Yeah, that's what they tell me," I shot back sardonically as he shook my hand.

"Lana, this is Noble Richmond," Jae said. "He's been with the Resistance for years and has stepped in to fill the gap left by Christine's… absence."

The name made me pause, and I scrunched up my brow, pulling an old line of text from the recesses of my mind. "'*But, tell me, where is princely Richmond now?*'"

Noble cocked his head. "Excuse me?"

Akio chuckled behind me. "Shakespeare. *Richard III*. Nice pull, kitten."

71

I blushed, feeling a bit like a pretentious ass. If Akio was complimenting me, that probably meant I was being one.

"He's a character from *Richard III*," I explained to Noble. "Called Richmond. Your name made me think of him."

"Oh yeah?" The wiry man considered that for a moment, still gripping my hand tightly. "What does he do?"

A smile flitted across my face. "Well, he wins in the end."

Noble's answering grin was fierce. "Then I'll take it."

CHAPTER 9

I PLUCKED my hand out of Noble's grasp, not quite ready to be so chummy with him yet.

"So painting me on the sides of buildings—is that part of your strategy for winning then?" I asked pointedly.

He chuckled, broad dimples forming in his cheeks. "Your men warned me you might not like that. But there wasn't time to ask for your permission. And of course, we weren't even sure at that point whether you'd return to us alive."

Fen growled at those words, the sound so like a wolf that I actually glanced over to make sure he hadn't shifted.

Noble's gaze shot to him, his look assessing. Then he lifted his hands and backed away from me, walking around the table again to resume his seat. He gestured for us to join him, and we pulled out chairs on the opposite side of the table.

"I understand if you don't like my methods, Lana." He leaned forward, already seeming antsy in his seat. I wondered why he'd bothered sitting at all. "And I understand if you're not happy about being thrust in the spotlight. But if can be perfectly blunt, you were standing center stage already. I just turned the light on."

My brow furrowed. "I don't—"

"Did you think your name wasn't being whispered in Blighted households all through the Outskirts? Or being spoken of in hushed voices by Gifted and Touched in the Capital? You are of both worlds, and both sides want to claim you. There has never been another person like you."

I squirmed uncomfortably under his intense gaze. "Yeah, so?"

"Whether we like to admit it or not, if this rebellion is going to have any hope of succeeding, we need magic on our side. And we need more Blighted to join our fight. I believe you can help us achieve both of those goals. You can unite people."

His words made sense, and despite myself, I couldn't help liking Noble. With Christine, I'd always felt a bit of a disconnect —we were on the same side, but something about her had always grated on me. But the man before me, who moved animatedly in his seat as he talked in an impassioned voice, drew me in. When he spoke, I wanted to believe him.

Don't trust anyone more than they give you reason to.

My gaze flicked to Akio, and I was surprised to find him watching me instead of Noble. I lifted an eyebrow and tilted my head slightly toward the new Resistance leader in a silent question, and Akio nodded.

So the incubus was willing to give him a chance. Maybe I should too.

I turned back to Noble, resting my elbows on the table and leaning toward him. "You've got a point. But if uniting sympathetic Gifted with the Blighted is your aim, there's something much more likely to do that than 'The Crow.' Like the fact that it was a Gifted man who caused the Great Death."

Noble froze. But while his body remained motionless, his internal tempo picked up speed. I swore I could actually see him vibrating. Finally, he sat back, scrubbing a hand over his face. "You have proof of this?"

"No, not exactly. I mean, Rain came out and admitted it to me when he had me captured, but all that does is make it my word against his. I don't have any physical evidence that he was behind it."

"Rain Blackshear? The Chief Advisor?" Noble pushed his chair away from the table, circling around it to lean against the back.

"That's the guy. He's a fucking lunatic. He tried to pull magic from people en masse, and he's planning to do it again."

Noble let out a low whistle. "*Is* he now?"

"Yeah. He has some kind of machine run by magic, and it just needs the power of one more strong Gifted person. He said he has to wait in between pulls, to let the spell build back up again or something. That's why he kept me for so long. But if he needs magic from one more mage, that means he'll have to find someone to replace me. Once he does, we'll have maybe a week before his device is ready."

"And when it's ready? What happens then?"

I sucked in a lungful of air. "Then he tries to steal magic from the remaining Gifted population. Or most of them, anyway."

My heart pounded dully in my chest as I waited for Noble's response. Waited for him to tell me that wasn't our problem, that it was about time for the Gifted to suffer like the Blighted had. Those were all thoughts I'd had once upon a time—but I couldn't think that way anymore. And I didn't think it was just because I had magic now.

Noble chewed his bottom lip for a second. "Then you better

find a way to prove—beyond any doubt—that he's behind this. And soon."

I blinked at him. This guy kept surprising me. Not lingering on my shock, I glanced around the table at my four. "How? We just got chased out of the palace for even daring to suggest such a thing. I'm not exactly going to be allowed into any more council meetings. The Representatives made their choice. They stuck their heads in the sand and sided with Rain."

Jae spoke up from my right. "There are one or two who could possibly be convinced, but she makes a good point. We've been labeled traitors by the Representatives. There's no way they'll grant Lana another audience... not that she asked for one today." His lips twitched toward a smile.

I grinned, before I remembered that was the second time I'd tried to speak to the Representatives rationally, hoping for a reasonable response. When would I learn what a fucking waste of time that was?

Noble's fingers drummed restlessly on the back of the heavy chair. "First things first—find a piece of solid evidence of Rain's guilt. Without that, none of this matters. Once you do, you can find a way to show it to the Representatives."

"Find a way?" I snorted. "I was worried about getting jumped by guards when I was technically allowed to be there. Now that I'm the new symbol of the Resistance and almost got arrested for disturbing a council meeting, I don't think we'll make it two steps into the palace."

"You may not have to." Noble paced a few steps away then turned back. "There's a rumor that Rain is going to be moved up from his position as Chief Advisor to Representative soon; he'll be given Representative Lockwood's old seat."

"*What?*" My chair scraped against the dingy floor as I shot to my feet. I felt Jae's cool hand cover mine on the table while Corin rested his large palm on the back of my neck. Blowing out a breath, I let my head drop, blood still simmering. "What?"

"I'm not sure whether they ever actually intended to let you have the seat. Theron Stearns is a stickler for tradition, so maybe he would have. But after your disappearance, things shifted. Rain's been angling for a seat on the council for years."

My jaw clenched. I wasn't mad about Rain stealing the position from me; I didn't want the fucking thing. If I never set foot inside the People's Palace again, that would be just fine with me. But I hated to think of him advancing higher in the ranks of the government because of Beatrice's death, profiting yet again from his murdering and scheming.

"Okay, so that's just one more disaster we have to stop," I ground out.

Noble belted out a laugh, leaning over his side of the table toward me. "I wasn't thinking you'd 'stop it' so much as 'crash it.'"

I blinked dumbly. "Crash it?"

"Several years ago, when Victor Kruger took over the seat for his late father, there was a—"

"Public ceremony." Jae spoke slowly, his fingers tightening around mine. "He was introduced to the people from the grand terrace of the palace. Crowds gathered on the lawn."

"Exactly." Noble's dimples reappeared as he grinned. "Not a bad place to unmask a villain, is it?"

Jae's expression was far less enthusiastic. "It could work. It would be incredibly dangerous though. We'd be surrounded by Gifted, not to mention palace guards and all the Representatives."

The grin slipped from Noble's face, a look of intense seriousness replacing it. "That's why you'd better find compelling evidence. You'll have to make them listen before they attack."

Oh gods. Judging by the way today had gone, that would give us about half a second to get their attention before they decided to kill us. What the hell kind of evidence could we find that was *that* compelling?

"So when is the ceremony?" I asked, my brain still churning over ways to prove Rain's guilt. Too bad we couldn't just roll that giant ball of magic down the mountainside and show it to people. But even though Rain had said he couldn't access it, couldn't transfer it into himself, the magic clearly wasn't dormant. And I didn't know what would happen if we disturbed an object with that much raw power.

Noble interrupted my thoughts by answering the question I barely remembered asking. "Two days."

I choked out a laugh, sinking back down into my chair. "Two *days*? We're supposed to get irrefutable evidence that Rain caused the Great Death in two days?"

Noble chuckled mirthlessly. "Two days is pushing it, to be honest. We need to move fast. I don't doubt your assessment of Rain's timeline, but we're all just making educated guesses. If we're wrong, and he's further ahead than we think... well, let's not get caught with our pants down."

Fuck. He was right.

I nodded, finally putting my finger on why I liked him more than I'd ever liked Christine. Noble treated me as an equal. Christine had always done that grating thing so many of the Gifted did, addressing me as "Ms. Crow" but somehow twisting the formality so it sounded like an insult. Noble knocked ideas around with me, listened to what I had to say, and wasn't afraid to admit he didn't know everything. All marks of a solid leader, in my opinion.

"Okay. We'll start digging for evidence." I rapped my knuckles on the table. "Shit, maybe Beatrice has something at her house. I never got to check her office after the bomb went off, but I doubt she would've kept anything having to do with her suspicions about Rain at the palace anyway."

"Good. Let me know what you dig up, and if you need more manpower, let me know that too. I've got dozens of new recruits itching for something to do. It's no use trying to explain to them they'll see enough fighting to last a lifetime soon enough."

Noble's voice grew heavy with his last words, and I peered at him curiously.

He didn't look much older than I was, maybe twenty-nine or thirty. But he spoke like a battle-worn general, one who'd seen more of the world's evil than a single person should.

I wondered where he'd come from, what scars in his past had shaped the man he was today. I was starting to realize we all had them, and that even wounds inflicted years ago could still bleed.

"Thank you, Noble. We'll stay in close contact." Jae stood, the other three men rising with him.

My four dipped their heads respectfully to Noble, and I followed suit before we turned toward the door. Pausing with my hand on the doorframe, I threw a glance over my shoulder. "Hey, don't work too hard to make me a legend, all right?"

I was half-joking, but his response wiped the smile from my face.

"Don't worry, Lana. I doubt I'll need to. I have a feeling The Crow will fly high all on her own."

My heart thudded like a drumbeat in my chest as we stepped quickly down the stairs and headed for the guardroom. Much as I hated to admit it, I had a sneaking suspicion he was right.

And that terrified the hell out of me.

CHAPTER 10

GRAY EYES.

My father's eyes.

And green. I hadn't known it, but my mother's eyes were green.

The photo under my fingertips blurred, the gray and green both melting into a wash of color as tears welled in my eyes.

Gods. I resembled my mother so much, it hurt my heart to look at her. Was this what Beatrice had felt when she gazed at me and saw my parents in my features? The mingling of bittersweet joy and sharp pain, her soul recognizing a part of itself at the same time it realized that part no longer existed?

It fucking sucked.

But I couldn't stop looking at the pictures.

I sat cross-legged on Beatrice's bed, flipping through an old photo album. Every image I saw was a new revelation about a life I'd never known. I wished more than anything I'd had the guts to sit down and do this with my grandmother while she was still with me. I wanted someone to tell me stories about these pictures, to give them context and make them come alive.

I sighed. *And if Beatrice were here, maybe she could tell us whether she had any damning evidence against Rain hidden away in her house, or if all she ever had against him were unverified suspicions.*

A soft knock startled me, and I straightened, wiping the back of my hand across my eyes.

"Come in!"

The door opened a crack, and William poked his head in tentatively, his shaggy red-brown hair sticking up in all directions. His eyes were like saucers, almost as big as his mother's always appeared behind her glasses.

"Um, Miss Crow? We found some more boxes."

Beatrice's estate was enormous, with dozens of rooms and even more hidden storage areas. And she appeared to have kept every important document she'd ever had—and especially every trinket, token, or picture from before the Great Death. The prospect of going through it all was daunting, so I'd asked my impromptu houseguests to help us with our search.

It had taken a few gentle nudges to get them comfortable enough to touch any of her stuff, let alone go through it. But once the kids got over their nervousness, they threw themselves into the task as only eight-year-old treasure hunters could.

We'd unearthed a plethora of papers, pictures, heirlooms, and books.

But so far, nothing to do with Rain.

"Thanks, Will. Do you want to bring them up here? Are they too heavy?"

"I can manage." He puffed his thin chest out, and I smiled despite the worry clamped around my heart like a vice.

The official announcement had been made the day after we visited Noble. Rain would be presented to the people of the Capital as their newest Representative later today.

And we still had no proof.

The young boy slipped out of the room, and I dropped my head, staring at the photo album that sat on the bed before me. I could get lost in these pictures of my parents, not much older than I was now, happy, in love, and so full of hope. But that wasn't helping. I needed to find out something about Rain, not my—

I blinked.

Gray eyes.

Just like in my dreams.

"My dreams," I murmured, though only the walls could hear me. "Holy fuck. My dreams!"

Leaping off the bed, I dashed out the door and hurried down the stairs so fast I almost missed a step. Wheeling around the corner into the sitting room, I blurted, "It's me!"

My four looked up from their various positions around the room, where they pored over old notes and papers. Ivy peered over Jae's shoulder as he sorted through a neat stack.

"Uh, yeah it is." Fenris cocked an eyebrow at me. "Hey, killer."

"No!" I was gasping for breath, my brain moving too fast for my mouth to keep up. "It's *me!*"

"We need more, kitten." Akio was stretched out on the couch, lounging like a model as he shuffled papers around on the floor in front of him.

"The evidence we're looking for. It's me!"

Corin ran a hand through his short blond hair. His eyes were a bit glazed over, and he looked exhausted. None of us had gotten enough sleep the past few nights. "Didn't we already decide they wouldn't take your word for it? You can tell them exactly what Rain told you, but it'll just be your word against his."

"No, it won't! I saw something. I must have. When I was a kid!"

Several blank stares greeted me, but Jae's green eyes glittered with interest. "Saw what?"

That gave me a moment's pause.

"Well, I don't know, exactly. I don't remember. But that dream I keep having about my father—the one where he gives me the ring with the magic suppressing spell on it? It must be based on a memory. And in one of the versions of that dream, Rain was there. When he captured me, Rain told me he shared his plans with my father. I think I saw something, some part of that exchange. That's what my fucking brain has been trying to tell me all this time!"

Akio sat up gracefully, swinging his legs off the couch. "No offense, kitten, but how does a memory you *think* you have help us prove anything?"

I shot him a triumphant smile. "Because we know someone who can access forgotten memories."

Marielle Arcand definitely remembered us.

At least, her frosty expression made me assume so. The first time we'd come here, she'd been coolly polite, but her demeanor today could best be described as "coldly rude."

"Oh. You."

That was her only greeting as she let the door slam shut

behind her. She stalked across the pristine lobby toward us, and Jae took a step forward, his posture defensive—as if he needed to protect me from this waif of a woman. Then again, she *was* one of the most powerful witches in the Capital, and she didn't like me at all. So maybe I shouldn't scoff at his protectiveness.

He might've also been extra jumpy because we'd left the other three members of our team at Beatrice's. We'd decided it was safer, since Akio was now openly known as a Resistance member, and Fen and Corin probably were too. But not having them with me made me feel like I was missing a limb.

"Yeah. Us."

I matched her tone, squaring my shoulders. I would've been able to look imperiously down at her if she hadn't cheated by wearing four-inch stilettos that elevated her to my eye level. Her black hair was pulled back in a slick bun again today, and she was even thinner than I remembered.

Marielle sighed, rolling her eyes elegantly—however the fuck that was possible. "What do you want?"

"We need another memory potion."

She arched a brow, pursing her red lips. "Having fun digging up the past, are we?"

I scowled. "Yes. *We* are. And *we* can pay, if that's what you're worried about."

"It's not," she said shortly.

Dear gods, give me the patience not to drop-kick this fucking witch.

Ratcheting up my inner calm, I slipped my hand into Jae's, trying to absorb some of his tranquil energy. "Well then, will you help us or not?"

Marielle regarded me in silence long enough for me to notice her receptionist smiling smugly from behind the counter. What that woman had against me, I didn't know. Except maybe that I'd dared to bring a Blighted man into this upscale establishment last time I came.

Before I could start a fight with the smirking receptionist, Marielle nodded sharply.

"All right. But my fee is tripled."

My heart almost stopped. *Six thousand dollars?* Shit. I didn't have it. I could cover maybe four, but my last visit here had put a serious dent in my nest egg. Beatrice had plenty of money, but I didn't know how to access it, or if she'd even left it to me. So much had been going on I hadn't sorted any of that out.

"I..." I tried to hide the flush creeping up my cheeks. "I don't—"

"That's fine," Jae said smoothly.

Squeezing his hand, I shook my head, but he squeezed back harder.

"It's fine, Lana. I shouldn't have let you pay last time. I have family money that I wish I didn't. This will be the best thing I've ever spent it on."

My pride wanted to argue with him, but my practicality wouldn't let me. We needed this potion, and we needed it now. And somehow, the idea of letting someone else help me wasn't nearly as terrifying as it'd once been. I knew the lengths I'd be willing to go to for my four, and it seemed unfair not to let them do the same for me.

"Thank you, Jae."

Impulsively, I tugged on his hand and leaned up to press a kiss to his cheek, so close to his lips I felt his breath as he inhaled.

His clean scent filled my nostrils, what I imagined an ocean breeze might smell like. I felt more than heard the hitch in his breath, and I had to drag myself away from the warmth of his skin, the slight roughness of his stubble.

When I turned back to Marielle, she looked even more annoyed than she had a minute ago. I guess public displays of affection were beneath her too.

Without another word, she turned sharply and led us to the back, through the hallways bathed in red light, to a small room with a cauldron hanging from the ceiling.

"You want another potion like the first?" she asked, pulling items out of the cabinet and arranging them on the small workspace. She lit the flame beneath the cauldron using her magical fire starter then shot a glance at me.

"Yes. Except a more powerful one, if that's possible."

"How so?" She turned to face me, her expression less hostile now that I was offering her an interesting challenge.

When I explained what we were looking for, she considered for a moment then nodded. "I can do that."

I breathed a sigh of relief. There were dozens of ways this plan might fail, but at least we'd passed the first hurdle.

Marielle set to work on the potion, grinding up several ingredients with a large stone pestle before dropping them into the cauldron. Jae and I watched her in absolute silence as she began to stir and chant in a low voice. As tempted as I was to fuck with her just to see if I could make actual steam come out of her ears, we needed that potion more than I needed to indulge my petty childishness. Besides, I had enough challenges to overcome without adding "getting hexed by a witch" to my list of problems.

It took all my self-control not to start fidgeting as minutes ticked by and the stirring and chanting went on and on. Had it taken this long last time? Probably. I'd been antsy then too, but I'd also been distracted by the news of Rat's death. Now there was nothing but Jae's hand in mine, the sound of Marielle's spoon scraping the bottom of the cauldron, and her low voice intoning words I couldn't understand.

By the time she finally finished, I had teeth marks embedded in my lower lip. She used a long tube to extract the liquid from the cauldron, pouring it into a small vial before stopping it up with a cork.

Jae handed over a black credit card, and Marielle smiled genuinely for the first time since she'd greeted us. Once she'd processed his payment, she dropped the potion into my waiting palm.

"A drop in each eye, two drops in the ears, the rest in your mouth," she instructed me.

"Really?" I grimaced. I'd gotten a whiff of the thing while it was brewing, and it had *not* smelled potable.

She scowled. "If you want it to work, yes."

My stomach dropped. I'd gotten much more comfortable with magic since discovering it was a part of me, but twenty-four years of old habits were hard to break. The idea of ingesting something made of magic sent a nervous chill skating over my skin. What if she'd brewed it wrong?

"It won't kill you," Marielle snapped, correctly interpreting my silence. If she was slightly less hostile, her words might've been easier to believe.

Still, I closed my fingers tight around the potion and nodded. "Thanks."

The witch waved her hand at us in a clear dismissal, and Jae ushered me through the door and back out to his car. As he pulled away from the curb outside Mélange, I pressed the stone on my earring to activate my communication charm.

"Did you get it?"

Corin's voice sounded in my ear so quickly I was sure he must've been waiting for my call.

"Yeah. We just left Marielle. We're on our way to the palace."

"Not without us, you're not."

"Corin—"

"No, Lana. It wasn't worth us coming to get the potion with you, but if you're heading into danger, we're all going to be there."

"That doesn't make any sense! The palace is the least safe place for you to be right now."

Even as I spoke, I noticed Jae turn the car away from the palace—and toward Beatrice's house. I shot him a glare, but he avoided my eyes.

"It won't be much safer for you, but you're going anyway. So are we." Corin's voice had taken on the stubborn edge that meant his mind was made up. I knew that tone well. He might be the only person I knew who was more pigheaded than me.

"Sorry, killer," Fenris threw in. "But you only get twenty percent of the vote, and I think you're outnumbered on this one."

"Well, Jae is on my—" I started, but cut off at the slight shake of the mage's head.

"We need to stick together, Lana. I bought some potions and enchanted weapons Corin and Akio can use if it comes down to a fight."

Damn it. My stomach twisted, worry for my four just barely edging out my desire to have them with me. I wouldn't change our situation for the world, but sometimes I hated having four pieces of my heart exist outside my body. It was nerve-wracking as hell.

I sighed. "Fine. But if you come, then we *stick together*. We all go, we better all come back."

"We will." Corin's voice was firm.

My heart squeezed painfully. If only that was a promise I knew he could keep.

CHAPTER 11

JAE DIDN'T DRIVE DIRECTLY UP to the palace, as he had on numerous other occasions. Instead, he left the car several blocks away, and we approached on foot. Peacekeepers lined the palace grounds, directing curious residents of the Capital onto the sweeping front lawn before the palace.

It was packed with people. The only areas that were free of crowds were the large fountain in the middle of the lawn and the angled roads leading up to the palace entrance. The roads were currently blocked off. Three red banners bearing the emblem of the Order of Magic hung from the balcony that spanned a section of the palace above the grand entrance doors.

We pushed our way through the crowd, which grew even thicker toward the front. I stayed close to Corin, worried that the people around us might notice a Blighted man in their midst. But there were so many different kinds of magic mingling in the air it was hard to pinpoint their exact source, so his lack of magic was much less obvious. The size of the throng made it easy for us all to disappear.

On the balcony, Theron Stearns stood next to Rain. The two men were backed by the remaining five Representatives, and Jonas Nocturne stood off to one side. Whether he was there as part of the ceremony, or in an official capacity as the Minister of Justice, I wasn't sure. Given the size of the crowd, I guessed it was the latter. He was likely on duty, coordinating the activity of the Peacekeepers and palace guards.

The Secretary General's voice was magically amplified to carry over the entire crowd as he expounded on Rain's years of service to the country, his dedication to magic, and his efforts to improve life for the Gifted.

My heart pounded dully in my chest. Yeah, that sounded about right—plus or minus a little genocide.

Akio took the lead, somehow managing to part the crowd for us without shoving and elbowing people aside like I would have. When we were nearly to the cordoned off road, and as close to the front of the palace as we were going to get, I slipped the potion out of my pocket.

A drop in each eye, two in the ears, the rest in the mouth.

I swallowed. There wasn't a single part of Marielle's instructions I liked.

"Here goes nothing." I looked at Jae. "You ready with the amplification spell?"

He nodded grimly, his green eyes serious.

Popping the cork out of the small vial, I held the bottle over my eye, trying to ignore the dark red color that was reminiscent of congealing blood. I tipped a drop into my left eye, then my right.

It burned.

My vision swam, everything around me turning a hazy red color. Quickly, I tilted my head and applied drops to both ears.

The liquid slithered inside my ears, seeming to worm its way deep into my skull. I threw back the remaining liquid like a shot of whiskey.

But godsdamn—whiskey never burned like *this*. My eyes stung, my ears felt muffled, and the liquid coated my tongue, tasting like copper and some pungent herb I couldn't identify. It slid down my throat, leaving a scalding trail in its wake.

I opened my mouth to curse, but all that came out was smoke.

It poured from my eyes and ears too, thicker and darker than the wisps of smoke that had come from Gerald, rising high into the sky above me. My knees gave out, and I felt strong hands grab me from behind, supporting me as my body sagged and my head tilted back.

Disorientation flooded me. I wasn't sure I was still breathing. I couldn't feel air entering my lungs, just smoke pouring from me in an endless stream.

"Lana." Jae's voice came from a world away. "Did you see your father with Rain that day? Did you see Rain confess his plans to steal magic?"

And I remembered.

The memory slammed into me with the force of a speeding car. Then it continued through me, flowing out of my body and into the smoke swirling above my head. I saw the scene play out in my head as I heard it magically amplified all around me, drowning out Theron Stearns' words.

My father stood with his back to me as I peered around the door of his study. A younger version of Rain paced before him, his eyes burning like fire, his movements erratic.

"Think of it, Dominic! Where will it stop? If this continues, in just a few generations, everyone will have magic. And what will magic be worth then? Absolutely nothing!"

My father shrugged his broad shoulders. "I see your point. A lineage of pure magic means less than it used to. But there's nothing to be done about it, Rain. This is the way of the world."

Rain's face lit up with manic excitement, and he grabbed my father by the shoulders. "It doesn't have to be."

The older man chuckled uncomfortably, brushing the grasping hands off his shoulders and stepping back. "What do you mean? What grand theory have you cooked up this time?"

"Not a theory. A plan. And I've finally found a way." The frenetic energy Rain had been giving off stopped, his focus seeming to narrow down to a pinpoint as he grew unnaturally still. His careful mask of sanity and civility slipped, and for a moment, I could see the monster inside. "We'll take magic away from those who don't deserve it, and give it to those who do."

His words hung in the air for a moment. My father let out another choked laugh as tension stiffened his shoulders. "You can't be serious, Rain. You can't take magic away from people who were born with it. And who would decide who 'deserves' it?"

"I would. And I can. I will." Rain's voice was soft, his body like a statue. "Help me, Dominic. I'm almost ready. I just need—"

"Rain, be serious! What you're talking about is dangerous. Insane. Not to mention impossible."

"Not impossible. I've found a way." Rain slipped a hand into the inner pocket of his suit jacket and withdrew a small glass orb, no bigger than a marble. Inside, a pure white light glowed. I could feel the power contained in that tiny ball of light even from where I hid behind the door, peering through the crack in the hinge.

Silence fell. My father reached out toward the orb, but then arrested the movement. "Is this...? Have you truly...? What have you done?"

"This is magic." Rain's chest rose and fell rapidly. "This is one man's magic, harvested from his body and contained in its purest form. Once I

replicate the pull on others, I'll be able to redistribute the power as I see fit. Will you help me?"

"No," my father murmured. Then he repeated more forcefully, "No, I won't help you."

Rain blinked. "I... thought you understood."

My father scoffed. "I understand your frustrations. I understand wanting to prize and value magic, to preserve the bloodlines of pure magic users. But this? This is unconscionable. This is theft of a person's very essence. I cannot—"

There was a crack, and a harsh blast of wind threw him backward. It pinned him to the bookcase, sending bits of paper flying. Before my father could fight back, Rain swept from the room.

I ducked behind the door as he passed then darted into the study, fighting the wind that still howled in the room. A moment later, it cut off abruptly, and my father stumbled forward. He caught himself in a crouch and stood slowly, a dark look overtaking his features.

Anger. And fear.

Until that day, I'd never seen my father afraid.

A noise escaped me, halfway between a squeak and a sob, drawing his attention. His jaw tightened, and he reached for the tungsten and copper ring on his pinky finger, pulling it off and clasping it between his palms, muttering the words to a spell.

Shouts and screams filled the air, and I looked around, wondering how so many people had gotten into our house.

No. Wait.

They weren't here.

And neither was I.

I blinked and gasped, drawing a heaving breath into my lungs. Smoke still hung heavy in the air above me, and the shouts and cries were coming from the crowd around us.

Akio and Fen were behind me, holding me up. My feet were

still on the ground, but I wasn't supporting any of my own weight. Red still tinged my vision. Nausea roiled my stomach.

I looked over at Jae, almost choking on my words. "Did... did it work?"

He nodded, his mouth set in a grim line, and we all turned toward the balcony where the Representatives stood.

Theron had stepped back from the railing a few paces, and he pivoted slowly to face Rain. He'd cut off the spell amplifying his voice, so I couldn't hear what he was saying. But he gestured angrily. Rain shook his head, arms held out in a supplicating gesture.

Olene stepped forward from the line of Representatives, speaking urgently to Theron. The Secretary General nodded then turned toward Jonas, gesturing again toward Rain.

Thank the gods. They believed me.

They had to. They'd heard the truth themselves, seen the demented look in the mage's eye as he ranted to my father. Seen the ball of pure magic he had pulled from another human being.

Relief flooded me as Rain shrank back from Theron. The Representatives may have been complicit in the violence and subjugation that followed the Great Death, but at least none of them were as evil as Rain. And now that they could no longer pin the blame for it on the Blighted, they would have to make reparations. They'd have to—

It happened so fast my mind didn't process it until it was over.

One moment, Rain was stumbling away from a towering Theron, and the next, a thick bolt of electricity flew from his hands toward the Secretary General. It struck the white-haired man in the chest, and Theron stumbled backward. Another blast threw him against the balcony railing, and he pitched headfirst over the side, tumbling to the steps below.

The screams around me ceased like someone had hit the mute button.

I waited, stinging eyes held wide, for Theron to rise. To fight Rain, to order the guards to attack.

But he didn't. His dark form on the palace steps didn't even stir.

He was dead.

"How…?" My voice was hoarse, and my throat burned at the single word.

"No. It shouldn't be possible," Jae murmured slowly. "The Secretary General wears protection charms. Always."

Rain raised his hands toward the other Representatives, the threat clear. The guards on the balcony had stepped forward, tense and alert, but nobody moved to attack him.

Fuck. Rain may not have performed the second magic pull yet, but he must have already begun testing the transfer of magic into a new host. And clearly, it had worked. The day we'd confronted him in the council room, his magic had seemed different, stronger somehow. I'd thought it was just because of his agitation, but I was wrong. He'd increased his powers.

Light danced around both of his outstretched hands, and I swore I could feel the electric charge in the air from yards away. Slowly, a translucent shield formed in a tight dome around him.

Then he spoke, and this time his raspy voice echoed out over the crowd, louder than Theron's had been.

"Dominic Lockwood didn't share my vision. Theron Stearns didn't either. But I tell you now, my vision for the future *is* coming. And in that future, all defenders of pure magic will have a place of honor! They will be granted power beyond their wildest hopes. They will be the preservers of magic, and all who are without it will bow before them." He swept his arm out, encompassing the crowd. "You all have a chance, right now, to join me and secure your place at my side. Or you can resist—and become Blighted yourselves."

His booming voice died out, and in the brief silence that followed, my gasping breaths were all I could hear.

Then, slowly, Victor Kruger stepped up to Rain's side. Nicholas Constantine followed, a wide grin splitting his face. A moment later, Jonas Nocturne stepped to his other side. A shocked cry escaped my lips, and Jae's shoulders stiffened.

As soon as he came to a halt beside Rain, Jonas nodded to the guards surrounding them. Several of the uniformed officers shifted toward the remaining Representatives, their posture threatening. Either the guards were loyal to Jonas, or they'd decided to take Rain up on his offer. Or both.

"Oh shit." Fen's voice was low. "What do we do now?"

Before I could force my frozen lips to answer him, chaos erupted around us.

CHAPTER 12

SEVERAL BURSTS of magic flared to our right as a group of Gifted turned on the people around them. Screams filled the air again as those under attack fought back or dove for cover.

On the balcony, Olene moved. She threw her hand out like a whip, and several green balls of light flew forward and stuck to the translucent shield around Rain. A half-heartbeat later, they exploded, weakening his shield. She repeated the move once more before two demon guards grabbed her from behind, wrestling her back.

Rain let the shield drop entirely, but that only freed him up to attack. He raised both hands above his head, bolts of electricity sparking between them, just as Simon Gaunt turned tail and ran. The older man was halfway to the arched doorway in the palace wall when the lightning struck him in the back. It propelled him the rest of the way, sending his body hurtling into the doorframe. He hit the ground and didn't get up.

Olene was putting up a valiant fight. The two guards who'd attacked her lay at her feet, and she stepped over their bodies to go after Rain again. The brown-haired mage shouted something to Jonas and jerked his head toward us. I swore his gaze found mine for a moment, even though it was impossible at this distance. But my stomach dropped anyway.

As Victor, Nicholas, and Rain battled against Olene and Eben, Jonas called the remaining guards to his side then leapt off the balcony. But they didn't fall like Theron had. They dropped gently to the ground, slowed by a levitation spell on Jonas's part.

When they landed next to the Secretary General's prone body, none of them spared it a glance. Jonas descended the steps with a heavy stride, and it wasn't until he and his posse of guards started to cross the street toward us that I shook myself out of my stupor.

"They're coming for us! Rain must've given him orders to collect us. Or kill us."

I stepped out of Akio and Fen's supportive grasp, not pleased to find that my legs wobbled as I moved forward. The memory spell had fucked me up. My vision was no longer streaked with red, but I felt fuzzy and disoriented.

"We need to get out of here. Lana, you have the transport spell?" Jae turned worried eyes to me before glancing back at his father.

"Yeah." I shook my head to clear it. "Yeah, here."

I dug into my pocket for the small cylinder, dropping it on the ground at my feet.

"Lana! Watch out!"

Corin pulled me out of the way of a blast of ice that had gone wide of its target as two Gifted men traded blows nearby. My heart pounded in my chest as he righted me. Between the Gifted civilians around us and the posse of Representatives headed toward us, we were sitting ducks.

"Thanks," I breathed, giving his arm a squeeze before turning back to where the transport charm lay.

Shit. Where was it?

My eyes scanned the ground, panic rising in my chest as I searched for a glimpse of the small object.

Jonas gestured, and a puff of purple smoke exploded several yards away. The transport spell. He'd levitated it away when I dropped it.

And now we had no way out of here.

As Jonas and the guards reached the palace's front lawn, they fanned out into a curved line with the Minister of Justice front and center. Without breaking stride, he raised both hands, and two massive fireballs appeared above his palms. He made a slicing gesture, and an arc of fire flew toward us.

"Fuck!"

I dove out of the way, but not fast enough. The fire caught my shoulder, seeming to cut and burn at the same time. Pain flared, but I shook it off as I rolled and regained my feet.

Jae threw a ball of blue flame at his father, his beautiful face a mask as he attacked his own flesh and blood.

The blazing orange flame flashed again as Jonas hurled a blast to deflect the blue fire. As he did, the guards at his side splintered off, charging for us. Two shifted as they ran, leaping toward us as a tiger and a wolf.

Fen shifted in a burst of light. I followed suit, meeting the snapping jaws of the attacking wolf with my own sharp fangs. We broke away and circled each other, and a thought occurred to me. Could I still do magic while I was in wolf form?

Summoning the power inside me, I called up a huge gust of wind, striking the wolf in the side. He staggered, and I pounced, my teeth ripping into vulnerable exposed fur.

Blood flooded my mouth, the coppery taste urging on my animal instinct to fight. I tore my mouth away and leapt over the wolf's still body, growling at a warlock who advanced on me.

But before I could attack him, a blade flew past me and sank into the man's chest. Shock registered on his face even as he pitched sideways.

"Well done, kitten. You distract them with your fierce growl and I'll kill them," Akio drawled behind me, another knife already in his hand as he faced off with a red-skinned demon.

I huffed, licking blood from my muzzle. *He shouldn't be allowed to call me 'kitten' while I'm literally a wolf.*

Ha! Fenris's bark of laughter echoed in my head as he and the tiger circled each other. *I'll be sure to tell him that.*

Before I could respond, the tiger leapt.

Fenris!

The two shifters rolled in a blur of orange and gray, powerful jaws snapping and claws bared.

I've got this, killer. Help Jae!

Shit. I swung my head around wildly. Corin and Akio were fighting the demon together, but Jonas kept throwing scorching arcs of fire their way, making them dive for cover. Jae tried to stop him, flinging blast after blast of blue flame. His father was good though. He blocked each attack, seeming to predict Jae's movements almost before they came.

Of course he did. He was probably the one who'd taught Jae how to fight.

Not announcing my entrance into the melee, I threw my own fireball at the older mage. The smooth motion of his hands was interrupted as he jerked one arm up to block the attack, barely defending himself in time.

Jae shot me a grateful look, and the two of us pressed our advantage, driving Jonas back a few feet.

A sharp call rang out behind me, and I glanced over my shoulder.

My blood chilled.

The guards and Peacekeepers who'd been stationed at the edges of the palace grounds had finally reached us. Dozens of them now raced our way through the rapidly thinning crowd.

How had this many of them sided with Jonas? With Rain?

"Shit! Jae! We've gotta get out of here!"

A burst of light in my periphery called my attention back to Jae's father. I didn't turn in time to block his attack, but Jae threw a ball of fire to intercept it. The two magical flames collided so close to me I was blown off my feet. I landed flat on my back, the impact jarring my already shaky body.

Jae rushed over and grabbed my hand, pulling me to my feet. My muscles and bones protested the quick movement, but I ignored them.

"I need you to hold off my father. Can you do it?" Jae was breathing heavily, his green eyes wide.

Unable to speak yet, I nodded.

"Good. *Don't* try to take him down. Just keep him distracted for a few minutes. And be ready to run when I tell you."

Jae's words barely made sense to me. Run? Run where? We were surrounded by palace guards.

But I didn't bother to question him further. Instead, I stepped forward and flung a dagger at Jonas. The sudden switch to a nonmagical attack caught him by surprise, and he was late with his block. The dagger struck him in the shoulder, making him howl in pain. The two balls of fire burning above his hands flickered out.

Unfortunately, even without the flames, he was far from helpless. He raised his good arm, and I was lifted off my feet, my body suddenly moving toward him.

Godsdamn it! The fucker stole my move!

I twisted and writhed, trying to slow my forward progress, but I had nothing to push against. I couldn't resist the magic pulling me.

So I did the opposite. Conjuring a huge gust of wind behind me, I drew my dagger as I was propelled forward like a shot. I caught sight of Jonas's wide eyes before I slammed into him, my blade sinking into his side.

Blood welled over my hand, and I felt his body jerk. He shoved me away, but I didn't fall backward. Instead, his levitation spell lifted me higher into the air before slamming me back down to the ground with a painful thud. Jonas repeated the action a few more times, lifting my body and beating it against the ground like a child taking out his aggression on his least favorite toy.

I tried to use my forearms to absorb the worst of the impact, but on the third rough landing, my cheek smacked painfully against the ground. Stars exploded in front of my eyes, and my brain felt like it was rattling around in my skull.

Finally, he let my body drop and didn't pick me up again. There was no time to recover though. A half second later, a flash of light flew toward me. I rolled out of the way, and a fireball hit the earth where my prone form had just been, leaving a scorched black trail across the grass.

With one hand pressed to his bloody side, Jonas advanced on me. He threw another blast of fire. This time, I countered with my own, but the flame was weak, barely holding his at bay.

"Jae! Whatever you're doing, do it faster!" My voice betrayed my panic, but I was beyond caring. This fight was about to end, and I wasn't going to be the winner.

"Almost there...." Jae's voice was strained.

Yellow light flared under the hand Jonas held to his abdomen. He was already healing himself.

Fucking great.

Jonas gestured with his other hand. My body slid toward him, dragging across the rough ground.

"Jae!" I scrabbled for purchase, uprooting chunks of grass as I slid by. But there was nothing solid to grab hold of.

"*Now!*"

At Jae's shout, strong hands wrapped around my ankle, tugging me back. The spell still pulled me forward, but another set of hands joined the first, and my forward motion stopped. A potion sailed over my head, striking Jonas in the chest. He snarled as it began to eat through his once-pristine suit, sending up a trail of smoke as it devoured the fabric. When it reached his skin, his snarl turned into a roar of pain.

Corin pulled me backward, half dragging, half carrying me. I looked over my shoulder. Jae was crouched on the ground, his head bent low as he hovered his hands over a shimmering blue portal.

"Hurry... I can't keep it open long," he ground out.

Not hesitating, Corin and I leapt into the portal. The world spun in a stomach-wrenching way as we passed through the blue glow and "down" suddenly became "sideways." We emerged from a portal in the wall of a house, landing roughly on our backs as our initial downward momentum shifted.

Corin rolled me out of the way in time to avoid getting crushed by Akio as the incubus came through after us. He somehow made the strange perspective shift look like nothing, landing gracefully on the floor in a crouch. Fenris sailed past him in wolf form and skidded to a stop on the beat-up hardwood. He shook out his gray fur as Akio crawled away from the portal and hauled me to my knees, patting me down roughly for injuries.

"*What the hell were you thinking?* You could've gotten yourself killed going after Jonas like that."

I wasn't badly injured, just bruised and exhausted, but I didn't pull away from his touch. "Jae told me to distract him."

Akio raised one perfect eyebrow, his hands still roaming my body. "Kitten, you and I need to have a serious discussion about what constitutes a distraction."

Before I could respond, Jae appeared through the portal behind us. He hit the floor hard then twisted immediately, throwing a hand back toward the portal to close it.

Not a second too late.

A pair of legs in the blue and white uniform of a palace guard were halfway through the portal when it snapped shut. The two polished boots fell to the floor with a quick *thud-thud.* Bile rose in my throat, and I choked back my disgust. At least the wound looked like it'd been cauterized immediately, so there wasn't a lot of blood. But still. Fucking gross.

"Holy shit! Jae, did you—?"

My voice cut off.

Jae lay limp on the floor, his eyes closed.

His chest unmoving.

CHAPTER 13

"JAE!"

I scrambled over to him, mirroring what Akio had just done to me as I ran my hands over his still body, searching for mortal wounds.

There were none.

Just a few scrapes, but no sign of a life-threatening injury.

I looked up, my eyes wild. "What the fuck happened to him?"

Akio's face was grim. "He opened the portal too fast. Portals aren't like transport spells; they require opening a hole in the ether. It would normally take several hours to create the gap gently, without tearing anything. But we didn't have time for that. Jae just ripped through the fabric of existence, and the blowback hit him hard."

Oh fuck. I pressed my mouth over Jae's and blew. Then I started doing chest compressions, falling back into old Blighted habits in my panic.

I exhaled into his mouth again, hating that this was the first time my lips had ever touched his. My heart thudded sluggishly in my chest like it was made of lead. Several people rushed into the room, but they weren't attacking us, so I paid them no attention.

"What does that mean? Is he injured? Can I heal him?" I peppered Akio with questions as my joined hands pressed hard against Jae's chest in a steady rhythm.

"I don't know, kitten. But… try. Please try."

Desperately pretending not to hear the fear in his voice, I drew on the magic inside me, trying to clear my adrenaline so the power could flow through me unimpeded. I reached out with my magic, feeling for Jae's life force.

It was there, but faint—barely stronger than Beatrice's was after that bomb decimated her office. Pushing away my worry that I'd fail to save Jae just like I'd failed Beatrice, I let my magic flow into his body, piecing together the holes in his life force. It was much more difficult than any healing spell I'd done before, because there wasn't an obvious physical injury to heal. His life had simply been nearly snuffed out.

I kept doing chest compressions while I worked, not caring if applying Blighted first aid made me a disgrace to mages everywhere. All I cared about was keeping Jae alive.

When I felt his heart start to beat on its own beneath my hands, my skin went numb with relief. I blew out a shaky breath and looked up at the men gathered around me. "I can heal him, I think. But it's going to take a while."

"Fen, help me." Corin slipped an arm around Jae while Fen— back in human form—took his other side.

They carried him over to a bed in the corner and lay him down gently. I followed close on their heels, eager to resume my ministrations. Now that I could breathe again, I spared a glance at my surroundings. We were in a sparsely decorated bedroom in what looked like a rundown house. It reminded me of my apartment in the Outskirts, but older and bigger. A dusty smell hung in the air, and the room was empty except for the bed and several large boxes in the corner.

The sheets were clean though, and wherever we were, it seemed safe.

As I sat down on the bed and rested my hands on Jae's chest again, I picked up whispered voices behind us. They were too low for me to hear everything they murmured, but I was certain I heard "The Crow" mentioned several times.

This must be a Resistance cell in the Outskirts, separate from the main base I'd visited every other time. Fen had said they were branching out as they gained new recruits, and Jae must've decided it was safer for us to come here than risk leading his father to the Resistance headquarters.

Fenris broke away from the small group and came to stand behind me, leaning down to press a kiss to the top of my head. He spoke into my hair. "We need to tell Noble what happened right away and find out what he knows. Will you be all right without us for a bit?"

I nodded mutely, never taking my eyes off Jae's elegant, too-still features.

Fen drew in another long breath, the warmth of his lips making my scalp tingle, and murmured, "We'll take care of this. You just take care of Jae. I know you can, killer."

Corin pressed a kiss to my temple, and Akio ran a finger lightly down my cheek, and then the three of them left with the Blighted resistance members who'd rushed in to meet us.

The door shut softly behind them, and silence swallowed the room. While I was glad for the chance to concentrate on healing Jae, the quiet also gave me too much space to think.

And I didn't want to think.

Didn't want to think about how Rain was one step closer to his goal.

Didn't want to think every semi-decent member of the Representatives was likely dead by now.

Didn't want to think that Jae's own father had sided with Rain, and that he'd tried to kill not just me, but his only son.

I'd never considered myself naïve. In fact, the word I would've more likely used to describe my personality was "jaded." So why did I keep finding myself surprised by the depths people would sink to in their pursuit of power?

I didn't want to consider the odds we were up against, or how small a force fought on our side.

I didn't want to contemplate our odds of success.

So I shut all those thoughts out. Instead, I poured my focus into healing Jae. His chest moved softly beneath my fingertips as I worked, rising and falling with deepening breaths. I gazed at his face, entranced by his fine features—the long nose and high cheekbones above a strong jaw and slightly pointed chin.

His thick eyelashes fanned over his cheeks, and even with the lids lowered, I could picture the exact emerald green shade of his irises.

Jae couldn't fucking die. He was one of the best men I knew. Someone who hadn't let his upbringing or the world he was born into define him. A man who had questioned everything he was told and shaped himself based on his own beliefs.

I loved him.

The realization calmed my heart, and the magic began to flow through me more easily, almost rushing from my body into his.

I love him.

I'd probably loved them all on some level since that first day I woke up and found myself tied to Akio's bed. But this was more than that. I loved *him*. And it didn't matter to me anymore whether my feelings originated from the bond or not, because in this moment, I knew beyond a doubt they belonged to me.

Running one hand along the side of his face, I gently brushed his hair back. A moment later, those green eyes I knew so well blinked open slowly, and a sigh fell from my lips like a prayer.

"Lana… are you all right?" he asked weakly.

I snorted. "Why do you always ask me that after your dad does something awful to *you?*" And then, because I didn't want him to feel bad for worrying about me, I added more softly, "Yes, I'm fine. Are you okay?"

Jae sat up gingerly, scooting up on the bed to lean against the headboard. "I will be." He rubbed at his chest, as if still feeling the after-effects of his heart lurching back into motion. "I knew opening a portal that fast was dangerous. I haven't done something that foolish in years."

I moved up to sit beside him, clasping his hand and continuing to feed the healing spell into his body. I wasn't sure if my sudden wave of emotion earlier was the cause, or if Jae was sending magic back into me, but I could feel my own injuries repairing themselves. The bruises from Jonas's attack faded slowly from my body.

We sat in silence for a few moments while Jae regained his strength and I tried to think of what to say.

For some kinds of grief, there were no adequate words.

"It doesn't make any sense, but I'm almost relieved."

Jae's soft words brought me out of my reverie, and I glanced at him. "What do you mean?"

"I've always seen the kind of man my father was. From as early as I can remember. But still, despite every piece of evidence he gave me, I still held out some hope. That I was wrong—that he would change."

"And now?"

He closed his eyes briefly. "And now I know. I wasn't wrong. He'll never change."

"I'm so sorry, Jae."

"You have nothing to be sorry for," Jae said bluntly. "He does."

My stomach tightened. "You know we're going to have to fight him."

"I am looking forward to it." His normally calm voice held an edge I'd never heard before.

I looked over at him, a lump forming in my throat. "It shouldn't be like this. You shouldn't have to fight your own father."

Jae's chest rose and fell erratically, making me worry for his heart all over again. "Maybe it shouldn't be, but it is. This is my fault. I've known what he's capable of, what he's truly like, my whole life. I should've stopped him a long time ago."

Squeezing his hand tighter, I pulled it to my chest. "Don't put that on yourself! His actions are his alone. You are *not* your father, Jae. You're everything he isn't—honest and empathetic and brave as hell. He doesn't deserve to have a son like you. And if you don't want to fight him, just say the word. Because I'm dying to."

I broke off then, pressing my lips into a thin line. I probably shouldn't have run my mouth like that, but my wildly fluctuating emotions were getting the better of me.

Gods. How fucked up is it to realize you love someone and offer to kill their father in the space of five minutes?

There was a pause as Jae regarded me, and for the first time, no part of his expression was unreadable. He looked younger and wilder with his calm facade stripped away, nothing but naked emotion on his face.

It was breathtaking.

But before I was done looking my fill, his lips were on mine.

He kissed like a starving man—like every pent-up emotion he'd held in for so long was finally spilling out into the connection between us. He wrapped his arm around me, and a moment later I was straddling his legs, our lips still locked in a hot, wet kiss. My hands framed his face as he sat up straighter, tasting my teeth with his tongue.

I moaned against his mouth, running my hands down his lean chest to his firm waist. I tugged up his shirt and slipped my hands under it, seeking the warm skin underneath and—

Jae's body stiffened.

He shoved me roughly away from him as he scrambled off the bed.

I thought for a second he was going to run out the door, but he paused a few steps from it, his breath coming in sharp bursts. A pair of bare light bulbs gleamed from an old fixture in the ceiling, and in their dim light, he looked like a trapped, wounded animal.

Embarrassment flooded my body. Shit. Had I been wrong? I knew Jae cared for me, but there were different kinds of love. Maybe the sparks that danced across my skin at even the most casual touch from him were mine alone.

I cleared my throat, my mouth suddenly dry. "Jae, I'm so sorry. I didn't mean to—"

"No. It's not you." His voice was harsh, his shoulders shaking from whatever emotion he was holding back.

I wasn't sure what was going on in his head. But I knew we stood at a precipice. He'd opened himself up to me in so many ways, but there was a part of him that had always remained closed off.

I'd given up hope of ever seeing it, considering the vice-like control he had over his emotions.

But I'd finally caught a glimpse of that hidden part of him.

And even though the intensity of it scared me, I wasn't going to let him push it back down.

CHAPTER 14

JAE'S BODY WAS TAUT, poised to run or fight, like a fox caught in the open on a desert plain. He looked like he was on the verge of breaking down entirely, and part of me wanted to back away, to give us both an out.

But sometimes, the only way out was through.

I stood slowly, keeping my eyes glued to his back. He tensed as I approached, and when I reached out to lay a gentle hand on his shoulder, his whole body jerked.

"What, Jae? Please tell me. I want to help if I can."

"I don't... I don't want you to see." His voice was rough, almost unrecognizable.

"See what?"

"Me." His shoulders slumped, and my heart broke.

"I *want* to see you, Jae. I want to know all of you." My words were soft, and he shuddered under my touch.

Slowly, I walked around to face him. He looked lost and pained; it was the same expression he'd worn at the Grand Ball after I met his father for the first time.

Deciding it was a better to ask forgiveness than permission, I pushed him slowly toward the bed. His movements were stiff, but he responded to my gentle guidance, stepping backward until he hit the edge of the mattress.

He sank down slowly. Keeping my eyes locked on his, almost drowning in the bright green of his irises, I deliberately moved my hands across his chest toward the first button of his shirt.

Jae seemed drunk, hypnotized by my gaze, and though he shifted uncomfortably, he didn't pull away as I undid the first button.

I continued that way, working my fingers down without ever breaking eye contact. When the shirt hung open loosely, revealing a small sliver of his chest and abdomen, I moved to push the fabric off his shoulders.

He stiffened again, reaching up to clamp one long-fingered hand around my wrist.

"Please, Jae."

I didn't push but held perfectly still until his grip on my wrist loosened. When it finally did, I slipped the white shirt down his arms.

A pained gasp fell from my lips before I could contain it.

This was what he hadn't wanted me to see.

Thick, pinkish lines streaked across his chest and shoulders— old wounds long ago healed over. What had caused these? A knife? A lash? Some kind of magic?

My gaze traced the lines across his body as I crawled up onto the bed with him. I followed one that disappeared over his shoulder, and when I saw his back, I had to force myself to keep breathing.

"Holy gods…."

His chest had borne a few scars, but his back was a patchwork of violence.

Unable to stop myself, I reached out a trembling hand and traced the lines of overlapping scars. Jae swallowed, holding perfectly still under my light touch. There was no deliberate pattern to them, just an array of slashes cutting across his back. They were thick, the reformed skin stretched over time. These wounds had been received when he was young, no more than a boy.

"Your father?" I whispered.

He swallowed thickly. "Yes."

"This was what you meant when you said you knew what kind of man he was." My voice was strained as fury and pity fought for dominance in my mind.

Jae didn't answer this time, just nodded slowly.

I wanted to scream. Wanted to hit something. Wanted to tear open another portal so I could go back to the palace and stab Jonas twenty more times—consequences be damned.

But my rage wouldn't help Jae.

From the looks of it, he'd had more than enough of that in his life. I didn't want to be the bearer of any more.

So instead, I leaned down and pressed my lips softly to a thick scar over his spine. His breath hitched, but I continued working my way across his back, pressing kisses of love and desire to all the places where his father had tried to break him.

As my lips worshipped him, his breathing slowly deepened and evened out. When I brushed them across the strong muscles of his shoulder, he let out a low groan.

The atmosphere shifted, the painful tension that had melted away earlier returning as something else entirely. Something that made my skin prickle with awareness and warmth spread low in my belly.

My heart pounded out a heavy beat as I sat back and climbed off the bed. Jae's deep green eyes watched my every movement, still a bit dazed. I crossed to the door and flicked the lock on the knob. It wouldn't keep out determined intruders, but it would grant us all the privacy we needed for the moment.

When I turned back toward Jae, butterflies took flight in my stomach as nerves unaccountably raced through me. The man before me had become one of my best friends, a guiding force in my life. His beauty and goodness were almost inhuman.

Actually, maybe *that* was why I was nervous. The things I wanted to do to him right now were very, very human.

But if we crossed this line, we could never go back.

I couldn't go back to being the thing he yearned for from a distance.

He couldn't go back to being someone I idolized from afar.

We'd each tumble from the pedestal the other had placed us on and meet on solid ground, our flaws and fears no longer safely hidden away.

Jae was the one currently shirtless, but his intense eyes made me feel completely exposed. My skin warmed everywhere his gaze roamed, as if it penetrated right through my clothes.

I approached him slowly and rested my hands on his bare shoulders, feeling the scarred texture of his skin under my fingertips. His hands came up to clasp my hips in a surprisingly possessive grip as he stared at me.

"Lana, are you sure…?"

I bit my lip. "How's your heart feeling?"

One corner of his lip twitched up, and his green eyes

lightened for a moment. "Good. Your healing skills are improving fast."

"Then yes, I'm sure."

Bending down, I pressed my lips to his. It was softer than our first kiss, gentler. An invitation and a reassurance all at once. The hands on my hips became almost bruising, and I felt the muscles of his shoulders bunch, but his mouth moved soft and slow against mine.

This was what I wanted, what I'd wanted for so long. Whatever pleasure there was in loving the *idea* of Jae, it was nowhere near as good as loving the man himself—scars and all.

As I explored his mouth with mine, I slid my hands down over the lean planes of his chest and stomach to his thighs. The muscles felt like steel as he tensed beneath my fingertips, but I didn't let that stop me.

Breaking our kiss, I licked and bit a path down his neck. Jae leaned back, bracing his hands on the bed, and when I showered kisses over the scars on his chest, his head lolled, his eyes falling half-closed. A bulge strained against the fabric of his pants as I dropped to my knees between his parted legs. He was already hard for me. I ran my hand over his cock through the fabric then gave a gentle squeeze, and Jae's head jerked up.

I could see him trying to wrest back control of his emotions, to put a lid on all the feelings coursing through him. To bottle them up like he always did.

But I didn't let him. I squeezed him through his pants again, stroking up and down his hard length, making his green eyes spark with desire.

Then I reached for his button and fly, inching them open to give me access to what I wanted. He lifted his hips to help me work his pants down a little, and a soft smile played across my lips. He wanted this as much as I did.

When his cock sprang free, the velvety softness in my hand made heat pool in my core. I stroked the warm, smooth skin gently, taking my time as I explored him.

This was Jae. *My* Jae. The man who had taught me, talked with me, and comforted me when I felt lost in a new world I didn't understand.

But now he was also the man who looked at me with fire in his eyes, who murmured soft groans and words of approval as I caressed his thick length. And I wanted this side of him as much as I wanted the cool, calm mage I'd come to love.

I dipped my head, exhaling hot breaths along his cock before running my tongue over the tip. He tensed and fisted my hair tightly but didn't try to control my movements.

The pull on my scalp sent another zing of pleasure through me, and I took him in my mouth, unable to hold back any longer. I wanted to feel him, to taste him. To make him lose control.

"Lana…." Jae dragged out my name as I swirled my tongue around him, his hips shifting in time to my rhythm.

I hummed in response, wrapping my hand around his base as I worked my lips up and down, loving the way I could feel him pulse in my mouth, growing even harder in response to my touch.

My gaze flicked upward, and the tempo of my strokes faltered.

Good gods. He's fucking beautiful.

Jae's head was tilted down, the muscles of his neck corded. His nostrils flared as he watched me, and his mouth dropped open slightly. But it was the expression on his face that undid me. The cool mask was gone, along with the doubt and pain that had broken through earlier. All that was left was raw, unfiltered desire.

Because of me.

A heady feeling of power rushed through me. I was on my knees before a man who never lost control to anyone. Except to me. I had cracked through his carefully erected walls, and as I sucked harder on his cock, those walls came crumbling down.

I licked his slit with the tip of my tongue, tasting his salty essence, and he bucked his hips.

The hand in my hair tightened, finally beginning to guide and control my movements. I let him, opening the back of my throat and pulling more of him into my mouth with each stroke.

He needed this. Needed to let go and take what he wanted.

"Touch yourself, Lana. Keep your mouth on me and touch yourself."

The rough, commanding edge to his voice was new and thrilling. I fumbled with the zipper on my jeans then reached my hand in to rub my clit, relieving some of the desperate ache building inside me. The rhythm of my mouth and tongue stuttered as my body tensed with pleasure, but I was more focused on his release than mine.

More than anything in the world at this moment, I wanted to make Jae come.

In a dusty room in an unfamiliar house in the Outskirts, with world-ending danger bearing down on us, all I wanted was to make him feel good. To make him feel loved.

My orgasm hit me like a freight train. I'd been so focused on his responses and reactions, trying to drive him over the edge, that my own climax caught me by surprise. But each moan from his lips, each muttered praise and curse, the radiant heat pouring off his skin—it all heightened my arousal until I couldn't contain it anymore. I flew apart with a muffled cry, struggling through the aftershocks to work him harder and deeper.

Suddenly, his hand on the back of my head stilled. His whole body went rigid.

"I'm coming. Oh gods, Lana, I'm coming."

Those words, in his strangled voice, were the most incredible sounds I'd ever heard. A heartbeat later, his cock pulsed in my mouth, thickening with his release. I swallowed greedily, not willing to let a bit of him go.

As he gasped for breath, I slowly drew back, flattening my tongue against the underside of his softening cock as I did, making him hiss and exhale roughly. I tucked him back into his pants and zipped them up, then adjusted my own clothes. Resting my cheek on his thigh, I looked up at him, sated and happy.

For a moment, his green gaze shone down on me, a brilliant smile lighting up his face.

Then his smile drooped, his eyes clouding over. "Damn it. I'm sorry. That wasn't what our first time together should've been like. With me half dressed, you fully dressed, in the middle of a crisis, in a room that…." He gestured vaguely around us, pulling away from me uncomfortably. "You deserve better than this, Lana."

What?

I tightened my grip on his thighs, not letting him get far. "*No*, I don't. I deserve exactly this. You. The real, true you, and everything that comes with it. And *this*"—I mimicked his gesture encompassing the room—"will always mean something special to me. Because it's the first time *this* happened." Rising up, I grabbed the back of his head and kissed him hard. When I felt him relax again, I softened the kiss and spoke my next words against his

121

lips. "This was everything I wanted. A moment doesn't have to be perfect to be amazing, Jae."

He cupped the sides of my face, delving into my mouth with slow, languid strokes of his tongue. When we broke apart, he rested his forehead against mine. "Gods, you're incredible."

I chuckled dryly. "If you think so, I'm not going to try to talk you out of it." I paused, regarding him seriously. "But I'm also a little damaged, and angry, and afraid. I want you to know those parts of me too. And I want to know all of you. Please don't hide from me—not the good parts or the bad."

Jae pulled me up suddenly, settling me on his lap and wrapping his arms around me, burying his face against my chest. His grip was crushing, like he was holding onto a lifeline. "I'm so fucking angry, Lana. I want to kill him."

I pulled him close, ghosting my fingers over the marks on his back before running them through his neatly trimmed brown hair. "I'll help."

CHAPTER 15

WE HELD each other for a while longer, and even as worry about what was to come beat against my chest, I reveled in the feel of Jae's body pressed tightly to mine.

No barriers between us.

No pretenses.

Finally, he lifted me off his lap and stood slowly. He stroked my cheek, gazing down at me with worshipful green eyes, then laced our fingers together and led me from the room.

The hallway we entered was dark and shadowed, but light glowed from the staircase at one end. A worn carpet covered the steps, muffling our footsteps as we descended. Voices reached my ear as we entered a small, mostly empty room. A wide archway on the left opened up into another room, and the voices cut off as we stepped inside.

Old furniture was spread around the intimate space, forming a rough circle. Noble was perched on the arm of a large chair next to a woman I didn't recognize. Fen, Akio, and Corin sat on a worn red couch, and several other Resistance members took up other seats in the room.

"Jae!" Noble stood and crossed to us quickly, clapping Jae on the shoulders. "Are you all right?"

"Yes, I am. Thanks to Lana." He shot me a smile, and Noble transferred his attention to me.

I wouldn't have thought it was possible, but the man's internal tempo was even faster than the first time we'd met. I half expected him to burst apart into pieces of pure energy at any moment.

"Well done, Crow. We're going to need you both more than ever. Rain needs to be stopped. Sit, sit! We're working on a plan of action." He paced back over to his chair and perched on the arm again.

Jae guided me over to a large armchair, mimicking Noble's pose by sitting on the side. He wrapped his arm casually around my shoulders, his thumb brushing my collarbone.

It was a gesture of intimacy and possessiveness he definitely wouldn't have made even yesterday, and I flushed slightly as all three of my other men noticed it. Corin and Fen didn't seem surprised—they almost looked pleased, actually. But Akio's face hardened, and he blinked several times, his jaw clenching.

My blush deepened, and I avoided his penetrating stare. I wasn't sure what his problem was with me and Jae, but now wasn't the time to get into it with him. Instead, I turned to Noble, who was speaking in low tones to the woman next to him.

"So, I'm assuming you were brought up to date on what happened at the palace?" I asked. "Do you have any updates? What happened after we left?"

He shook his head, scrubbing a hand down his face. "Nothing good. Rain Blackshear has taken control of the government and declared martial law. He's being backed by Victor Kruger, Nicholas Constantine, and Jonas Nocturne." His gaze shifted to Jae. "I'm sorry."

Jae dipped his head in acknowledgement. The mask of calm was back in place, but I felt his fingers tighten on my shoulder, and I was grateful he didn't try to hide his response from me.

"What about the other Representatives?" I asked.

"Theron Stearns is dead. So is Simon Gaunt. We think Olene Romo may have escaped, but Rain was able to capture Eben Knowles alive."

My jaw dropped. "Eben Knowles? Fuck. You mean Rain has one of the most powerful wizards in the country?"

"Unfortunately, yes." Noble's voice was grim. "Which means he's found a replacement for you, Lana. And that means—"

"The doomsday clock has started," Fen interjected with a frown.

"Godsdamn it. He could be doing the magic pull on Eben as we speak." My heart clenched as I thought of the old wizard. He'd been the quietest of the Representatives, and though I had no reason to suspect he was a good man, I'd hated him a lot less than some of the others.

"Yes," Noble confirmed. "And if he is, that gives us less than a week to stop him before he's ready to perform a large-scale magic pull."

"And we can't count on the Representatives to stop him. There's no fucking government left but Rain and his goons." I kicked at the threadbare carpet, my heart rate ratcheting up. "Gods, I can't believe how easily he demolished them. He's stronger than he used to be. Whatever kink there was in his first spell that wouldn't allow him to transfer magic to a new host, he's worked it out. And we have to assume that by the time we go after him, he'll be even more powerful than he is now. It'll take a fucking army to stop him."

The woman next to Noble spoke up. She had dark skin, a long neck, and hair so short it hugged her scalp. "Most of us can't fight him with magic. But we can be a first wave attack, distractions to keep him busy while those who can fight magically get into position."

I blinked. She'd spoken so straightforwardly it took me several seconds to realize what she was offering—that she and others like her would sacrifice themselves to give the rest of us a chance against Rain.

"You can't—"

Her look cut me off. "We're helping. One way or another, we're going to stop that son of a bitch."

Determination straightened her spine, and Noble dropped a hand on her shoulder. The girl's voice was light and musical, and when I looked closer at her, I realized she couldn't be much older than eighteen. The hardness in her eyes had fooled me at first.

I wanted to argue with her further but didn't know how. Could I tell her not to fight? I sure as hell wouldn't listen if our positions were reversed. But my stomach turned at the thought of what Rain would do to an army of Blighted men and women. Hell, with the new powers he was developing, he could probably take down an army of the Gifted without breaking a sweat.

And still, we had to stop him. Somehow.

I looked around the room at the gathered company. "We'll work together. Blighted, Gifted, Touched—there's power in numbers, and we all bring something to the table." I grimaced, turning back to Noble. "If we go in now, we've got a better chance of catching Rain off guard, before he fortifies his defenses even more. But then again, we'll also be going in blind, with no solid plan of attack. If we wait, we'll be more organized, but so will he."

A smile flashed across his face. "You think like a general."

Panic flared, but I pushed it back down. I wasn't the leader here. He was. I didn't want that kind of responsibility, couldn't be the one held accountable for the lives of all the Resistance members. Brushing off his words, I rolled my eyes. "I think like someone who doesn't want to get her ass handed to her by a super-mage."

"Agreed." Noble was still smiling fiercely, an expression that made him look a bit feral. "As to your question, I think we're better off—"

He was interrupted by another man entering the room. I recognized this one; he'd come to the war room to report to Christine once when we were there.

"Sir? We've got company."

The atmosphere in the room grew tense, the air seeming to thicken.

The smile slipped from Noble's face. "How many?"

"Two. Out front. They haven't broken through the concealment spell, but they're definitely trying to."

Noble nodded sharply then cocked his head at Jae and me. We rose smoothly, and I summoned a flame above my palm as we followed the Resistance member to the front door.

"You take the one on the left. I'll take the one on the right," I whispered to Jae. Then I stopped. "Wait. Should you be fighting this soon after almost dying?"

"If I could handle what you did to me upstairs so soon after a brush with death, I think I can handle this," he murmured back, his voice so low no one but me heard him.

I flushed but snorted a laugh. I'd always suspected Jae had a wicked sense of humor. It was nice to see him letting it out.

We peered through the small window in the door. A Gifted couple loitered on the cracked sidewalk outside the house, almost invisible in the gloomy evening light. It would be full dark soon, and there were no working streetlights in this neighborhood.

From what I could make out, they looked middle-aged and affluent. They also weren't being subtle about their presence at all. Were they Rain's soldiers? Some of his new recruits?

I shot a glance at Jae. "Don't go for a kill shot. We need to question them."

He nodded in agreement then gestured to Noble, who had his hand on the door handle. The Resistance leader twisted it suddenly and pulled.

We stepped up to the open door, careful to remain inside the concealment surrounding the house as we raised our hands in unison.

Maybe the couple somehow saw through the concealment spell. Maybe they sensed us.

Or maybe they were just out of better ideas.

Before I could hurl the ball of flame in my hand, the woman looked straight toward the house, and called out in a low voice, "Hello? We're looking for The Crow. Please, we want to join you!"

My arm froze in a cocked position, and I fisted my hand to put out the flame.

"Oh shit, killer! They're here for you!" Fen's loud whisper from behind us made me jump.

"Looks like our kitten's got a fan club," Akio drawled.

I dropped my arm and scowled at him over my shoulder. "Did you forget I know your weak points?"

Akio smirked, but stepped out of arm's reach. Smart man. I'd discovered a while ago that he was ticklish, and I wasn't above abusing that knowledge.

But at the moment, I had bigger issues to deal with. Like the Gifted pair in the street who were still swiveling their heads around, as if at any moment they'd catch sight of the house in their periphery.

They could be lying. Rain had taught me an unforgettable lesson about believing people too easily.

But Corin had taught me another lesson. Trust had to start somewhere if we wanted to move forward. Even Akio, who'd been given maybe the best reason ever not to trust another person again, had decided to give Noble a chance.

Trusting no one meant always being alone. And we couldn't win this battle alone.

Steeling myself against the urge to reignite my flame or at least pull a dagger from my thigh sheath, I stepped out of the house onto the crumbling front steps. As soon as I crossed the threshold, the couple's attention snapped to me.

"I'm—" I cleared my throat and tried again, hoping my words didn't sound as dumb as they felt. "I'm The Crow."

The woman's eyes widened. If she was disappointed by how I looked when I wasn't painted on the side of a building, she didn't show it. In fact, she appeared a little awed. "It *is* you. We... we've come to volunteer. To join the Resistance."

I glanced behind me. My four were crammed into the doorway, all looking extremely tense. Noble was slightly shorter than all of them, so I couldn't see him through the wall of muscle blocking the doorway. But screw it. He was the one who'd made me into "The Crow," so he could hardly complain about me making an executive decision on this.

"Come in. It's not safe out here." I gestured behind me, ignoring the tension radiating from the bodies at my back.

The couple darted up the steps quickly, casting furtive glances around them. The street was deserted, but I assumed at least some of the houses nearby were occupied. It really *wasn't* safe for us to be out here.

Grudgingly, the men stepped back, and as soon as the Gifted pair were inside, Noble closed and locked the door. He leaned back against it, arms crossed over his chest, watching the couple intently. Their eyes, however, remained fixed on me.

"Our names are Grace and Silvius," the woman began, a slight quaver to her voice. "We—we saw you on television today. We didn't go to the palace for the ceremony, but we were watching. We saw your spell, saw your memory. I can't believe...."

She broke off, drawing deep breaths as tears glistened in her eyes. The man, Silvius, wrapped an arm around her waist, picking up the thread where she had left off.

"We couldn't believe what the Chief Advisor did. All this time, we didn't know. We thought it was the—" He glanced at Corin, Noble, and the several Blighted Resistance members surrounding us. "Well, you know."

Tension thickened the air in the room. These Gifted might finally believe the Great Death wasn't caused by the Blighted, and they may truly be here to help us—but old prejudices died hard on both sides.

"We never attacked the Blighted," Grace said, her voice low. "But we didn't do enough to defend them when the Gifted mobs went looking for blood after the Great Death. We were still reeling

130

from what had happened." Her thin face was drawn, her eyes haunted. "The sickness struck so fast. A perfectly healthy person would be dead within hours, and so many people were falling. Bodies were left on the street. People barricaded themselves inside their houses, but it didn't help. We didn't know where it would stop, *if* it would stop. Or if it was coming for us all."

"I lost my entire family," Silvius murmured. "It's a miracle I still have Grace."

Grace gripped her husband's hand so hard her knuckles turned white. "We tried to rebuild our lives after that, to climb out of our shock and grief. We heard stories, rumors that the Blighted were to blame, but we never attacked them. We just... tried to get by."

Corin let out a muffled sound behind me, but he stifled whatever he'd been about to say. I could guess his thoughts though. "Getting by" was something the Blighted were intimately familiar with.

Grace licked her lips before continuing in a halting voice. "Last year, our daughter... ran away with a Blighted man. She told us she'd fallen in love with him and asked for our help. But we were afraid of what it would mean for her, afraid she'd be an outcast in society. We refused to help her. So she slipped away with him one night, and we never saw her again. We don't know if she's alive or dead, or—"

She broke off, covering her mouth as a sob burst forth.

"We lost our only daughter because we were too damn blind to see the truth," Silvius continued grimly. "We need to make it right. We can't undo the damage or make up for the violence against the Blighted, but Chief Advisor Rain needs to pay for what he's done."

"And you're willing to work alongside the Blighted to make that happen?" I asked, trying not to let suspicion color my tone.

"Yes. If—if you'll have us." Grace wiped her eyes with trembling fingers.

"We welcome your help." Noble stepped smoothly away from the door, drawing the couple's attention for the first time. "You're right. You can't undo the damage. No one can. But if you want to create a better future for your daughter, and for others like her, you've come to the right place." He grinned, his body practically vibrating with energy. "We're moving against Rain soon. And The Crow will lead us to victory."

My stomach soured. If there hadn't been two new Gifted recruits standing between us, I'd have kicked Noble in the shin— or the balls.

Fuck, that was a hell of a vow for him to make. Especially when he wasn't the one who had to live up to it.

But I affixed a confident look on my face and met Grace's watery gaze. "I will. I promise."

I bit my lip against the words that wanted to follow. *Or else to ruin.*

CHAPTER 16

"He shouldn't be doing that!"

"Relax, kitten, he's fine. Also, I'm pretty sure he can hear you."

"He can," Jae said calmly, though his eyes remained closed as he hovered his hands a few inches away from the peeling paint on the wall. "And Akio is right, I'm fine."

"But creating a portal is how you almost died yesterday!"

"Tearing open a portal *quickly* is what almost killed me. Creating one the right way is no more difficult for me than casting a concealment spell."

"I still don't like it." I paced nervously to the other end of the room, unable to watch the blue glow slowly spreading across the wall. "Why can't I do it?"

"She's got a point. Why can't she do it?" Akio watched me with glittering eyes from where he lounged on the bed.

When he'd flopped down onto it earlier, he'd paused before shooting me an inscrutable look. I swore he somehow knew exactly what had happened between Jae and me in the spot he now occupied.

Was that why he was being such a crabby ass?

"I *will* teach you how to open portals, Lana," Jae promised. "But a portal that takes me an hour to open now would've taken over six hours when I was first learning. The newer you are to it, the slower you have to go to stay safe, and we don't have time for that right now."

He had me there. With Rain only days away from being able to perform another magic pull, we didn't have time to waste. My four and I had all crashed in a slightly less musty bedroom downstairs last night, and I wouldn't have wanted to trade those six hours of sleep for six hours spent doing portal magic.

I sighed. "Fine. I understand. But please be careful."

Wrapping my arms around Jae from behind, I pressed a kiss between his shoulder blades, running my hands up his stomach and chest. I reveled in the feeling of his muscles relaxing under my touch instead of tensing like they had for so long.

A sound like a muffled growl came from the direction of the bed, and I gritted my teeth. I wasn't sure what had gotten stuck up Akio's ass, but he was in a damned pissy mood today.

Before I could call him out on it, Fen and Corin entered the room. I reluctantly dropped my hold on Jae so he could concentrate.

"How's the portal coming?" Fen asked, pulling me toward him and burying his face in my hair. I melted into his arms, letting myself bask for a moment in the scent of pine that always surrounded him. Maybe someday our lives could involve more of this, and less running, hiding, and fighting.

"Almost done," Jae murmured softly.

"Noble said he's heard from several other Resistance cells." Corin sat on the end of the bed near where we stood, catching my hand and running the pad of his thumb over my knuckles.

"They've all had people wanting to volunteer. A lot of Blighted, but Touched and Gifted too."

"I can't believe Rain hasn't lost the support of everyone in the Capital," I said bitterly, sinking down onto the mattress beside Corin and leaning into him.

He shrugged. "Greed and fear are both powerful motivators. As long as people are ruled by one or the other, they won't stand up to him. Whether they support him or not."

I gnawed my lower lip. I couldn't really relate to the lust for more power, but fear? I knew that emotion well. It didn't mean I wouldn't fight though. In fact, the more afraid I was, the harder I fought.

We'd decided it was too dangerous to leave the dilapidated house and risk exposure, so Jae was creating a new portal to the Resistance headquarters. We'd meet other cell leaders there and start to coordinate an attack on Rain—an undertaking that was finally starting to seem possible with our expanded numbers.

"There." Jae stepped back from the glowing blue patch on the wall. "It's small, but it's fully formed. It'll do for our purposes."

"I'll go tell Noble."

Akio rose gracefully from the bed and left the room without another word. As he passed through the door, my heart did a little stutter-step in my chest, already missing the feeling of rightness that came when my four were all near me.

Unbidden, the story he'd told me about Ria rose into my mind. Would he always resent me for the bond between us?

Trying to ignore the pit that opened up in my stomach at that thought, I followed Corin over to the portal, Fen right behind us. It was definitely smaller than usual—I had to hunch over to fit through it—but we emerged safely in the tunnels under the Resistance headquarters.

The guards who greeted us at the entrance kept shooting me awed glances, making the hair on my neck stand on end. It was better than the distrustful glares I'd gotten the first few times I came here... but not by much.

I hung back deliberately, and by the time we entered the large, crowded main room of the compound, Akio had rejoined us. I felt the heat of his gaze on me as we headed toward the war room.

The large table that dominated the room now surrounded by people. I didn't recognize any of them, but I assumed they were Resistance splinter-cell leaders and possibly new recruits. They stood as we entered. There was an awkward moment of silence as we all looked at each other before Noble burst into the room behind us and took control of the space.

"Thank you all for coming." He settled into the chair at the head of the table.

Several other Resistance members stepped back, gesturing for me and my four to take their empty seats. I hesitated, but didn't want to get this war council off to a bad start by denying their gracious offer. Besides, two of the men who stood were Gifted, and although it was a little, stupid thing, a Gifted man yielding his seat to Corin held meaning.

Noble drummed his fingers on the table as everyone got settled. The same girl who'd sat next to him yesterday was at his right hand today. As soon as our eyes turned to him, he leaned forward intently.

"The way I see it, we've got two possibilities for how to take down Rain. We can try to attack the palace, or we can bring the fight to the mountain hideout where he took The Crow. I'm not gonna lie to you—neither of those prospects will be easy. But we should do both. We'll use force against the palace, and stealth against his compound."

"Well, we know the palace is protected. How heavily guarded is the mountain bunker?" A Blighted woman with an eye patch over her left eye spoke up. A wicked looking scar emerged from the top of the black fabric, crossing her temple and intersecting her hairline.

"Very." I grimaced. "And probably even more so now that he's been exposed. When I was there, it was only guarded by spells and charms, but since Rain isn't trying to hide his plans anymore, I'm sure he's got real guards protecting the place."

"Right." She leaned back in her seat, pursing her lips.

"We need you to tell us everything you remember about the place," Noble urged. "Layout, protections, any weaknesses. Even if there've been changes, it will give us a base of knowledge to work with."

I nodded, and then launched into a description of Rain's mountain lair. Images from my escape flashed through my mind in vivid color as I spoke, chilling my blood. When I mentioned the ball of magic suspended inside the giant metal prongs like a glowing star, several jaws dropped and eyebrows raised.

By the time I finished detailing my escape, the room was quiet.

"I know it's daunting." Noble spoke into the silence, his voice infused with the same passion and energy he always exuded. "But it's what we're up against. We didn't choose it, and I don't know how we're going to do it, but we have to find a way to succeed. I, for one, am willing to die trying."

"Hear *fucking* hear." Eye patch woman raised her chin in agreement.

"The two of us can work together to break wards," one of the Gifted men who'd offered his seat said, nudging his friend.

The second man nodded. "We'll need backup, because it's time-consuming and draining. But if you can lead us to the wards, we can get them open."

"Excellent." Noble slapped his hand on the table, his eyes burning. "We'll send a small team into the mountains while the bulk of our force focuses on the palace. Once we destroy Rain's machine, we can deal with him. I'll lead the attack on the palace. We'll have a mix of Blighted, Touched, and Gifted fighters, so we'll need to team up strategically to maximize our advantage."

"I can work with a group of Blighted and try to find a weak spot in the palace's defenses. I'm good with a blade, and I can confound anyone who discovers us." A fairy with blue hair raised his hand tentatively. His magic flared as he spoke, and I saw everyone around the table relax slightly. Confounding was the flip side of a fairy's powers. While their magic usually made people around them feel unaccountably happy and at ease, they could also twist that magic to make people lose focus and motivation.

"Good. Good! What else?" Noble looked around the group, eyebrows raised.

Other hands began to pop up, new voices interjecting offers of help or thoughts on strategy. Noble's enthusiasm and determination kept the ball rolling, and I sat quietly for a moment, looking around the table at the people gathered here.

My soul knew four of them on the deepest level possible. But many of them were strangers to me. There were Blighted, Touched, and Gifted people spread around the table—not seated on opposite sides, but intermingled together. Talking to each other, listening to each other. All in pursuit of one common goal.

A spark of hope lit deep in my belly, burning low alongside the ember of my magic.

Maybe, *maybe* someday, things could be better.

If a future existed for any of us, if we lived beyond this week, maybe there was a chance we could create the world Rain had feared was coming. One where the Gifted and Blighted existed so closely together that the differences between them became unimportant. One where magic spread and thrived rather than being hoarded and fought over.

It was too much to wish for, too big a prayer. I knew that.

But still, I wrapped myself around that flame of hope, shielding it like a candle guttering in the wind.

I wouldn't let it go out.

Akio nudged me, pulling me from my thoughts. One corner of his mouth lifted in a smirk as he inclined his head toward Noble.

"What can you tell us about Victor Kruger and Nicholas Constantine?" the Resistance leader asked, repeating the question I'd missed. "Any weaknesses?"

I huffed a sigh, my mood plummeting. "Weaknesses? None that I saw. Unless you count being a major asshole as a weakness. I don't know what Victor can do, but Nicholas—"

I broke off as footsteps clanged on the stairs. A moment later, a young man rushed into the room, darting through one of the open spaces that had once held a floor-to-ceiling glass panel.

"Sir! Sir!" He stopped at Noble's side, gasping for breath.

"What is it, Justin?"

"You need to come, sir! You need to see! An attack—on a Resistance cell. They took—*everyone.*"

CHAPTER 17

NOBLE'S FACE FROZE.

For the first time since I'd met him, his internal tempo slowed, a starburst of pain flaring behind his eyes.

Then he snapped to full speed again, rising so fast his heavy chair skidded back, rocking on its legs.

"Where? Show me."

The boy nodded, his mop of black hair flopping over his forehead. Then he turned and darted down the stairs, Noble close behind him.

I shared a glance with my four and, as one, we stood to hurry after them. My heart tried to crawl up my throat as the stairs clanged under our feet, and when we hit the main factory floor, I broke into a jog, catching up to Noble.

The dark-haired kid led us to the barracks, where a group of people was gathered in one corner. He shoved his way to the front, and the crowd parted silently as we followed him through.

Next to a cot, on an overturned crate, sat a small battery-operated television. It had an antenna sticking out from the top and was so tiny and old-fashioned looking it was almost comical.

Or it would've been, if not for the grainy image displayed on its screen.

It wasn't a pavilion this time, but the palace steps.

And arrayed across those wide steps stood dozens and dozens of figures.

A Resistance cell, the boy had said.

An *entire* Resistance cell.

Most of the people were unbound, though several swayed on their feet with the telltale wooziness of someone wearing charmed restraints.

Mages stood all around them, boxing them in. Though the Blighted weren't restrained, there was nowhere they could go, nothing they could do.

Above them, on the same balcony where he'd killed Theron and wrested control of the government, Rain presided over the proceedings. Jonas, Nicholas, and Victor flanked him.

"There will be no tolerance for magic users who align themselves with the Blighted. And there will be only death for Blighted who threaten the rule of magic," Rain shouted, his raspy voice ringing loudly. "I promise you, there is room in my glorious future for any Gifted citizens who embrace it, who prove their worthiness. As for the rest—they are already as good as Blighted. Let them die together."

Nausea roiled my stomach, and I turned away from the television, slamming right into Akio's hard chest. I stared up at him wildly.

"A transport spell. We need to get a transport spell! We have to—"

"It's too late, killer. Look."

Fen's voice was hollow, and before I even glanced back, I knew he was right. My entire body resisted the movement, but I forced myself to turn around.

Rain walked to the edge of the balcony and pointed down at the people on the steps below. "These men and women are all traitors! I hereby sentence them to death."

He began to raise his arm, and I stopped breathing.

A movement from one of the prisoners caught my attention. It was an older woman with silver hair flowing past her shoulders. She must be Blighted. Her hands were unbound, her expression clear.

She dropped her head, and as she did, she raised her hands high in the air, her wrists crossed and her thumbs linked together, the fingers of each hand splaying out like—

Like a bird.

Like a... *crow.*

In a heartbeat, the gesture was picked up by those around her, everyone who wasn't restrained lifting their hands and bowing their heads.

Rain brought his own arm down swiftly, a snarl twisting his features.

The mages surrounding the prisoners sent jets of water streaming toward them. As soon as the liquid struck their bodies, it froze, encasing each captured Resistance member in a thick layer of glittering ice.

My heart hammered against my ribs so hard it hurt. I couldn't blink, couldn't look away. I stared at the prisoners arrayed across the palace steps, their bodies frozen in a final gesture of rebellion.

"No. We should have stopped it. I shouldn't have let this happen." My words were low and rough, forced out past numb lips.

"There was nothing we could've done. It was too late." Noble stood next to me, but neither of us looked at the other. His voice was thick with pain that mirrored mine. "Rain is baiting you. He's trying to lure you out, to make you come to him so he can fight you on his terms."

My breath stuttered.

Lure me out.

All those pairs of hands, held up in the symbol of a crow.

Rain was killing them to lure *me* out.

And they had gone to their deaths believing in me.

Bile rose in my throat, and I pushed my way back through the crowd, tears burning my eyes. I didn't care about the stares I drew, didn't care that I looked weak. Something terrible was building up inside me, and I needed to get out of here before it exploded.

I knew it made me a fucking coward, but I couldn't watch them die. I couldn't stay and witness those mages shatter the blocks of ice—see dozens of bodies fall to the ground like wet rags.

The tears were streaming down my face now, but it didn't relieve the pressure in my chest. I could barely breathe. Every inhale I took was short and ragged, burning my lungs.

I stumbled blindly through the Resistance compound, lurching through the common area and into a small, empty alcove. My knees wobbled, and I bent over, bracing one hand against the wall as I retched. Straightening slightly, I pressed my face against the rough wall, trying to ground myself as the world spun around me.

Hands caressed my back and hair; soothing voices whispered in my ear. But I couldn't listen to any of them, couldn't let myself relax into the calming touch of my four.

Those people were dead because of me. Because of a promise I'd made to them, a promise I had *become*, whether I wanted to or not.

But I hadn't wanted to. I didn't want any of this.

"Transport spell," I gasped.

"Lana, no. You can't go after him now. It's exactly what Rain wants," Jae argued.

"I won't go… to the palace." My stomach lurched again, my vision hazy from the tears that wouldn't stop falling. "I just can't be here anymore."

"Okay. Okay, killer." Fen cupped my cheek, his touch so gentle it made my heart squeeze painfully. I couldn't handle tenderness right now. "We'll get you out of here. But we're coming with you."

One of my four stepped away to find a transport spell.

I shouldn't have asked for it. The Resistance had a limited supply of them, and we would need as many as we could get our hands on for the upcoming fight. But what the hell—I was already a liar and a coward. Why not add selfish to the list?

Maybe once the rest of the Resistance members found out who I really was, how weak and afraid and unqualified I was for any of this, they'd stop following me. Stop idolizing me.

A few moments later, a small cylinder was pressed into my hand, the cold glass shocking my senses. I dropped it at my feet and shattered it with my heel as four pairs of hands supported me. Purple smoke enveloped us, and when it dissipated, the foyer of Beatrice's house came into view.

I pulled away from my men and stumbled up the stairs, heading for the far end of the sprawling house on the third floor. I wanted to be as far from any other people as possible right now. At the very end of the north wing, I pushed open a thick cherry wood door and slipped into what looked like a large study. A desk took up one corner, while a small couch and two chairs were situated in the middle of the room.

After kicking the door shut with my foot, I sank down onto the couch, drawing my legs up to my chest. No lights were on, but the curtains were only made of a thin cream-colored material, which allowed the warm glow of afternoon sunlight to filter in.

I wished I could turn it off and sit for a while in blessed darkness.

Maybe darkness would help me forget.

How the hell did Noble do this? Lead people into a fight knowing that even if we won in the end, many of them would likely die along the way? Was practicality about sacrificing a small number of lives to save many the sign of a good leader, or a bad one? I'd never been especially scared of dying myself, but the thought of risking other people's lives sent ice-cold fear spiraling through my belly.

I couldn't be responsible for that.

Except, I already was.

Pressing the heels of my hands to my eyes, I tried to snuff out the images of all those Resistance members, defiant even in death.

But their defiance hadn't helped. They were still dead. Gone.

A cry of anger and pain fell from my lips as I scrubbed my fingers roughly across my face. More tears spilled from my eyes, like a river flowing through a broken dam.

"Fuck," I whispered softly.

"That *is* often the best solution," a voice drawled from behind me, and my head jerked up. Akio lounged against the door. He must've slipped in while my eyes were closed.

"What do you want, Akio?" I asked, wiping the back of my

hand across my eyes. He'd joined the rest of my four in supporting me back at the Resistance base, but now that we were alone, I wasn't sure if he was here to mock me or comfort me.

"To see if you're all right." His tone was neutral, and his dark eyes glinted as he sat down next to me on the couch.

I laughed bitterly. "No! I'm not. And I realize it's selfish and horrible for me to be focused on how *I* feel when dozens of people just lost their lives. But I feel like shit, and I don't want to do this anymore. I'll fight beside you all. I'll fight Rain to my last breath if I have to. But I'm *done* being a leader, being a symbol. I don't want that responsibility. Let someone else do it."

"That's not how it works, kitten. You don't get to decide whether people believe in you."

My throat tightened, and I gritted my teeth against a fresh wave of tears. "They shouldn't." I shut my eyes, breathing deeply through my nose. "I know those people didn't actually die *for me*. But it feels like—"

"Oh, they absolutely did die for you, kitten."

I blinked slowly, staring up at him in horror. There wasn't a single thing he could have said that would've made me feel worse in this moment.

"What... what do you mean?"

He angled his head to look down at me. The warm light filtering through the curtains did nothing to soften his sharp features, and his face looked like it was carved from stone.

"Exactly what I said. You don't get a say in how other people feel. You may not want to be a leader, but if you act and people follow, you are one—like it or not." Akio's voice deepened as he reached out to stroke my cheek with the knuckles of one hand. "And you *are* a leader, Lana. You draw people to you like the North Star. They will follow you anywhere."

146

The rich, honeyed sound of his words poured into my ears like a sweet promise. My body came alive, my heart rate picking up as I found myself leaning into his touch, nodding unconsciously in agreement.

Then I froze.

Fucking hell.

I slapped his hand away from my face then shoved him so hard he fell back against the arm of the couch. Leaping to my feet, I stood over him, breath heaving.

"I told you, Akio! *Do not use your godsdamned incubus charm on me!*"

Before I could make a move for the door, Akio caught my elbow. "Kitten—"

I jerked roughly out of his grasp. "Are you going to charm me into leading the Resistance? Huh? Is that it?"

Instead of answering, Akio swept a leg out, catching me off guard and knocking me off my feet. I landed on my back with a thud, and the incubus was on me a moment later. His strong legs straddled me, his large hands pinning my shoulders.

"Is that what you think I'm doing?" he breathed, his eyes narrowed to slits.

"Yes!" I ground out. Our faces were inches apart, and I tried to ignore the weight of his body on mine, the way his spicy scent infiltrated my nostrils.

Hooking his arm and bucking my hips, I threw him off me. I scrambled to my feet, panting. As soon as he rose, I rushed toward him, my anger and hurt flaring out of control. My palms connected with the hard planes of his chest, shoving him back a step.

Fire sparked in Akio's eyes, and his body tensed. When I moved to hit him again, his hands whipped out like lightning, blocking my blow and controlling my wrists. He spun me quickly, driving me backward until my back hit the wall by the door.

His body boxed me in, his tight grip pinning my arms above my head.

I grunted and twisted in his grasp, lifting my foot to aim a kick to his insole. But before I brought it down, he leaned closer to me. His breath feathered over my face as his gaze burned into me like fire.

"You're wrong, kitten. I wasn't charming you." Akio's eyes were black holes that drew me in and wouldn't let me go. "In fact, I'll let you in on a little secret. I have *never* used my charm on you."

CHAPTER 18

His words caught me off guard, and I hesitated. I stared at him, breathing hard, as memories assaulted me.

Akio's mouth brushing the shell of my ear, his voice whispering my name. My body pressing into his unconsciously, melting against his large frame. The spark of fire that blazed all the way to my core at a simple touch or look from him.

It wasn't possible none of those things were because of his incubus charm. The feelings had been so immediate, so intense and undeniable. He *had* to have used his magic.

"Yes, you have," I insisted thickly. "I've felt it."

Akio's fierce gaze never left my face as he shook his head. He tightened his grip on my wrists, lips tilting up in a vicious smile. "No. I haven't. Sorry to tell you this, kitten, but whatever you've felt, whatever reactions you've had to me, they were all yours."

He spoke the last words like a challenge, a dare. They hovered in the space between us, stealing the air from my lungs.

Why had he let me believe he was charming me all that time?

For as long as I'd known him, I had never trusted my feelings for him completely, convinced they were manipulated or enhanced by his incubus charm. No matter how attracted I was to his dark beauty, I'd refused to give in to it. I'd been terrified of acting on an impulse that wasn't truly my own.

But if he was telling the truth, all those feelings I'd struggled with *were* mine. My body and soul's natural reaction to him.

And he'd fucking lied to me.

Without warning, I lunged forward, surging against his restraining hold on my wrists. My mouth crashed against his in a kiss that was more a war of teeth and tongues than a meeting of lips.

Not allowing me to get the upper hand, Akio shoved me backward again, slamming me into the wall as his tongue battled mine for dominance. His body rocked into mine, and I used the wall behind me as leverage to press closer to him.

When our kiss broke, he finally released his grip on my arms so he could pull my T-shirt over my head. But instead of removing it entirely, he left the sleeves wrapped around my wrists. He twisted the fabric sharply, gripping it tight with one hand to keep my arms restrained against the wall.

His other hand roamed my body with impunity, slipping down over my throat, massaging my breasts, sliding across the flat plane of my stomach before unbuttoning my jeans and shoving them down my legs. My panties followed, and the shock of cool air on my hot core made me gasp.

I worked my jeans off with my feet and kicked them away, my back bowing off the wall as I tried to bring my hips back into contact with Akio's. His large body pressed into mine again as he devoured me with another fierce kiss. Trapped against the wall, I wrapped my legs around his lean hips, trying to regain the upper hand.

Before I lost feeling in my fingers, he unwound my shirt from my wrists and tossed it haphazardly aside. Our lips broke apart as he pulled back slightly to stare into my eyes, the inky darkness of his irises as hypnotizing and mysterious as a swirling galaxy.

Why did he have to be so fucking beautiful?

And such a fucking asshole.

Torn between wanting to hit him again and wanting to kiss him until I couldn't breathe, I settled for grabbing a fistful of his shirt in each hand and yanking. The fabric of his soft, expensive tee ripped easily. I tore the pieces from his body, revealing the swirling black designs of the tattoos on his shoulders, pecs, and arms.

Giving in to the desire I'd had since I first laid eyes on them, I leaned down and let my mouth explore the intricate designs. I sucked and bit at the skin, leaving red marks in between the black whorls of ink.

Akio groaned, grinding his hips into me and fisting my hair.

He pulled away to work his own pants down, struggling for a moment because I refused to help him by loosening my legs from his waist. But finally, he pushed them down his legs, kicking them off after his shoes. When he backed me to the wall again, the only scrap of fabric separating us was my thin bra. His large cock pressed against my stomach, the heat of his smooth skin on mine spreading fire through my body.

He dipped his head and sank his teeth into the spot where my shoulder met my neck, just below the quartz necklace I always wore, and a blinding jolt of pleasure shot through me. The base of his cock rubbed my clit as he worked his hips against mine, and I moaned, already so close to coming I could feel my toes tingling.

But I needed more. I needed all of him.

I squeezed my legs around him, using that grip to try to work my way higher up his body, to bring his hardness to my entrance. I needed him inside me. Now.

Akio grabbed my thighs to stop me. His strong fingers dug into my flesh hard enough to bruise as he held me completely still.

"Fuck, Akio! Please!" My lips curled in a snarl as I struggled against his tight grip.

"I want to hear you say it, kitten." His tone was rough, the usually smooth timbre strained.

"What?" I grunted in annoyance, baring my teeth and biting at his lips.

"Tell me you want me," he murmured, like it was a threat. His voice was liquid sin, hardening my nipples and raising goose bumps across my neck.

"Fuck," I whimpered. My hips ground against him. Even though he wasn't inside me yet, I could feel his cock pulse.

"Tell me you want me," he repeated slowly. "Not because of some magical bond, and not because of my demon charm. Admit you want me because you just. Can't. Fucking. Stop yourself."

"Yes!" The cry burst from my lips as frustrated desire nearly blinded me. "Yes, godsdamn it, yes!"

Lifting my thighs in his powerful grip, Akio drew back and surged into me, filling me completely and slamming me back into the wall. We both cried out as he stilled inside me.

"Oh gods," I breathed, my head dropping forward.

Akio kept one hand on my hip, raising the other to grasp my jaw tightly. He tilted my face up, forcing me to meet his gaze. "Your gods can't help you now, kitten."

The dark promise in his voice sent a thrill of fear and desire through me, and I clung to him for dear life as he pulled back and plunged in deep again. My back chafed against the wall with each punishing thrust, but I hardly noticed the pain.

My body was on fire, burning for this man, on the verge of exploding like a dying star. I dug my nails into his back, scratching roughly, dragging my hands up his neck. I gripped the silky strands of his thick black hair, watching his face as he drove into me harder.

His impossibly beautiful features tightened with determination and desire as our bodies connected over and over. A sheen of sweat gathered on his brow, his usually perfect hair ruined by my fingers.

"I knew it would be like this. Your body wrapped around me so tightly, your thighs squeezing me, your breath and your moans in my ear." His eyes were hooded. His nostrils flared. "I knew it, kitten. From the very first moment I met you."

"What, you mean the moment I tried to kill you?" I breathed, taunting him even as I struggled to keep my eyes from rolling back in my head.

"Yes."

With that one word, he thrust into me so hard I swore we'd crack the plaster. Just like we had that first time.

His strokes grew jerky and uneven, and he reached one hand between us to strum my clit. His gaze bored into mine, a torrent of emotions raging behind his dark eyes.

Anger and pain.

Lust and love.

I knew all of those emotions intimately, because I felt them too.

My body clamped down around him when I came, as if trying to keep him inside me forever. I moaned and writhed, throwing my head back so hard it hit the wall with a loud smack.

Pleasure and pain mingled, and a bright white light edged my vision.

Akio dragged me away from the wall, perching me on the back of the couch. He wrapped both arms around my back and thrust into me deep and hard, the pressure sending sweet aftershocks through my sensitive clit. On his final stroke, he bent me backward over the couch. A stream of words fell from his lips in a language I didn't understand.

He ground his hips into mine for several more moments, as if unwilling to stop fucking me even as his cock softened inside me.

When he finally pulled out, I realized belatedly that all my muscles were shaking, my thighs sore from wrapping around him like a vice.

"Shit," I muttered weakly. "I'm not sure I can stand. I can't feel my legs. I can't even think."

Akio smiled wickedly, triumph flashing in his dark eyes. Then he plucked me off the back of the couch and dumped me unceremoniously onto the plush seat on the other side. My body bounced against the soft cushions as I let out a little shriek. Before I could sit up, he moved around and crawled over one of the arms, hovering above my body to claim my mouth in another soul-searing kiss.

He smirked against my lips. "See? I told you fucking is often the best solution."

CHAPTER 19

"Okay, *now* I can't feel my legs."

"Good." Akio chuckled, the sound vibrating through my back.

He was propped up against the couch, with me cradled between his legs. My head lolled on his shoulder, and I craned my neck to look up at him. "I guess maybe you were onto something with that fucking theory."

"Kitten, my thoughts on fucking are more than just theories."

Rolling my eyes, I reached around and dug my fingers into his ribs. An undignified giggle burst from his mouth before he grabbed my wrist in an iron grip, pressing his lips to the shell of my ear.

"Don't start something you can't finish, Lana."

Much as I'd grown to like his nickname for me, the sound of my real name on his tongue sent a jolt of pleasure straight to my core. I rubbed my body against him like a cat, basking in the knowledge that the feelings he sparked inside me were all my own.

"Wouldn't dream of it," I purred, as he slipped his hand under my shirt to cup my breast.

After our second, even more athletic round of sex, I'd insisted on getting dressed. I felt bad enough for having fled the Resistance base like a coward; the last thing I wanted was one of our fellow Resistance members walking in on me and Akio naked.

But I wasn't ready to leave the bubble of this room yet.

I had to, eventually. I knew that. Beatrice's house might seem like a haven right now, but if Rain wasn't stopped, there would be no safe place left in the world. Not even right by Rain's side, something his sycophantic followers didn't seem able to grasp.

Did they really think bowing to his will made them safer? It just made them temporarily less expendable than the rest of us.

As the euphoric high of mind-blowing sex faded, worry had come barreling back in to fill all the quiet spaces in my mind. But Akio had assured me Noble had things in hand for the moment.

Before we'd left the headquarters, he and the rest of my four had consulted with Noble. With the help of a few new mage recruits, the Resistance leader would make sure the remaining sub-cells were fortified from Gifted attack. Tomorrow, we'd solidify the final details of our plan against Rain and make our move. But this evening, we all needed to rest and clear our heads.

Sleep still felt a long way off though.

I placed my hand on his above my T-shirt, arresting the casual movement of his fingers on my nipple. If he kept doing that, round three was about to start any minute. And I had too many questions burning in my mind.

"Akio?"

"Yes, kitten?" His hand stilled, but he made no move to pull it out from under my shirt.

"Why did you let me think you were charming me for so long? You knew that's what I thought, and you knew I hated it. I flat out told you a bunch of times. So why not correct me?"

The incubus's sigh ruffled my hair. "After what happened with Ria, I swore I'd never let another person control me—through money, sex, magic, or anything else. After you attacked me and your magic flared, I felt something shift inside me. The moment I woke up from the blast, a pull drew me toward you. And it scared the hell out of me."

He gave my breast one last squeeze then splayed his hand across my stomach, pulling me closer into his body.

"Yeah," I murmured. "It scared the hell out of me too. My story isn't nearly as bad as yours, but I'm still plenty familiar with another person having control over me."

I felt Akio nod behind me. "The more time we spent with you, the stronger the pull toward you became. And the stronger it became, the more I resisted it. I suppose I let you think I was using incubus charm on you as a way to keep you at a distance. I saw how it made you distrust your feelings toward me."

"It did."

"And I thought if you didn't believe your feelings for me were real, perhaps I could convince myself my feelings for you weren't real either." His voice was serious, it's usual mocking tone gone.

"Yeah? How'd that go?" I asked teasingly, trying to lighten his mood.

"Not well. I alternated between hating you and loving you, wanting to force you out of my head one minute and obsessing over you the next."

"Huh. Sounds familiar." I chuckled mirthlessly, tracing a finger over the tattoos winding up his left arm. He hadn't put his shirt on when we'd gotten dressed, and for once, I couldn't blame his vanity. The scraps of fabric I'd torn off him were no longer wearable.

"I didn't want this." Truth resonated in his words, and even though I'd once been of the same mind, it still stung to hear him say it. "To be connected to another person like this. I didn't know how to handle it."

My heart ached. Burying my head against his neck, I inhaled the spicy scent of his skin. "I'm sorry, Akio. I don't want any of you to be bound to me against your will. I hate to even think of that. Maybe when this is all over, we can find a way—"

His hand tightened on my body, the other sliding under my shirt to wrap around me too, making it almost difficult to draw in air. "I said *didn't*, kitten. Past tense. I may still struggle with my history, but I can't imagine my world without you in it now."

Maybe it had been worry and not his tight grip squeezing my lungs, because I could suddenly breathe again.

My throat tightened around all the things I wanted to say, but I managed to murmur, "Same."

We sat in silence for a moment. The sun had set, and a large lamp on the desk lit the room with a dim glow.

"Why were you so mad at Jae? I noticed it when he healed me after we escaped Rain's compound, and again after I healed him and we…." I trailed off, glad he couldn't see my blush. "When we came downstairs, you looked pissed as hell."

Akio scoffed, shifting slightly beneath me. "It doesn't matter."

"It does to me. I care about all of you, and I don't want there to be tension between any of us. And that includes the two of you."

I felt his body tense. "I was… jealous. Not of the two of you together—I understand how the bond works. But I'd spent weeks struggling against my feelings for you and had finally begun to accept them. I just couldn't believe that repressed motherfucker came to terms with his feelings before I did."

A belly laugh burst out of me. "So you were just salty because you realized you were less emotionally mature than Jae?"

"I was *salty*"—he twined his legs around mine, engulfing my entire body with his—"because I saw what could be mine if I dared to reach out and claim it. And still, I wasn't sure if I could."

I closed my eyes, sinking into his warmth and strength. "I'm glad you did."

"Oh, kitten." The languid, teasing tone in his voice was back. "You have no idea."

My heart stuttered in my chest as I thought of what had brought him to this room in the first place. I didn't want to ask my next question, but I had to know.

"Did you... did you mean what you said before, or were you just trying to piss me off? About those Resistance members dying for me? About me being a leader?"

Akio sighed. "Well, as much as I enjoy seeing your claws come out, I—"

He was interrupted as the door flew open. Fen burst into the room, followed closely by Corin and Jae.

"Are you all right, killer?" The wolf shifter rounded the couch, dropping to his knees beside Akio and me, his warm brown eyes wide.

"Relax, Fenris. She's fine. Doesn't she look like it?" Akio drawled.

"I dunno. She's been stuck up here with your cranky ass for the last few hours. That'd be hell on anybody."

Akio muttered a foreign word under his breath, and I made a mental note to get him to teach me some Japanese curse words later.

"We held him off as long as we could. He's been pacing the kitchen for the last thirty minutes." Corin laughed, coming around the couch after Fen. He plopped down onto the plush cushions, reaching down to skate his fingers over the curve of my shoulder. "*Are* you all right?" he asked softly, his bright blue eyes shining with concern when I tilted my head to look up at him.

I nodded, pulling his fingers to my lips to kiss them softly. Though I was emotionally wrecked by the events of the day, this time alone with my men fortified me. The Resistance had suffered a devastating loss, but we wouldn't—we *couldn't*—let it stop us from fighting.

"So, what've you two been up to?" Fen asked, his playful smirk telling me he knew the answer to that already.

Rather than give him the satisfaction of seeing me blush furiously, or at the very least, to distract him from the redness of my face, I answered, "Akio was just trying to convince me I'm a natural-born leader."

"Oh." The wolf shifter pursed his full lips, scratching at the scruff on his cheek. "Well, you are."

"Ugh. Not you too." I groaned, sitting up straighter as Jae sank into a chair across from us. His foot reached out to tap mine, our bodies seeking even that small contact.

"If you're putting it to a vote, then me three," Corin chimed in.

I shot a pleading glance at Jae, but he just lifted one corner of his mouth, his green eyes dancing. "Sorry, Lana. Me four."

I scrunched up my face, the glow of pleasure at their faith in me warring with a hefty dose of disbelief. "You all have to say that. You're bonded to me."

"It's not just us, killer." Fen shifted to sit against the couch next to us, taking one of my hands so he could lace our fingers together. "We have the perfect excuse to follow you anywhere, but we're not the only ones who want to."

"He's not wrong." Jae leaned forward, resting his forearms on his knees like he always did when discussing something important. "I know you think Noble created your persona of 'The Crow' out of nothing. But the truth is, he did very little. You'd made yourself a legend through your actions without his help. People were already talking about you."

"But they didn't even know me!" I sat forward, mirroring Jae's pose unconsciously. "And I never met any of those Resistance members who died today. I never told them to do that. How would they have—"

"That's where you're getting confused, kitten." Akio's voice was teasing, but his words were serious. "Some people lead by telling others what to do, yes. But some lead simply by demonstrating a better way to live." He pulled me back into his embrace, strumming his strong fingers over my ribs. When he continued, he spoke softly into my hair. "I did mean it when I said those Resistance members died for you today. But not because you ordered them to. You didn't *make* them do anything. You simply fought for your beliefs so strongly that you inspired them to do the same."

His words and touch were a balm, calming the churning sea of emotion inside me.

And I thought maybe I finally understood.

It was terrifying to think of being responsible for other people's lives. The weight of that burden was almost too much to consider. But if I looked at it from another perspective, I could acknowledge the truth I hadn't been able to see before.

When it came down to it, I was willing to die fighting for a cause I believed in. Hell, I'd have some strong words for anybody who tried to take that right away from me. And those Resistance members today, our new recruits, Noble, even my four—they all had the same right I did.

The right to live and die for their beliefs.

So while I could acknowledge my part in becoming a symbol of the Resistance, perhaps inspiring others to join the fight, it wasn't fair to *them* for me to take responsibility for their deaths. Those who died today had each stood on the palace steps with clear eyes and hearts. They had made their own choices.

Every person who joined the Resistance made a choice.

My chest swelled with gratitude as I realized the strength and bravery of the people I had fallen in with.

I was proud of them.

It was an honor to be one of them.

And if it gave them hope in the face of terrifying darkness, I would lead them.

CHAPTER 20

"THESE ARE ALL the transport spells I could find, Miss Crow!"

William loped down the hallway toward me, his shaggy red-brown hair wild. Several glass tubes were clutched haphazardly between his small hands, and I took them from him quickly before he dropped them all.

"Thanks, Will." I slipped the transport spells in my pocket then ruffled his hair.

"You're welcome." He beamed up at me. "Are they going to help you fight Rain?"

Gods, I hope so.

"Yeah. They'll be a big help."

"Good." His face brightened even further, his thin chest puffing out with pride at having contributed to the fight.

My heart squeezed uncomfortably. I hoped like hell he'd still have that joyful, innocent look on his face tomorrow.

"We've got everything we need gathered," Retta said, coming up behind William and resting her hands on his shoulders, pulling him close to her.

Tears welled behind her thick glasses, and her hands shook slightly. Answering tears stung my eyes, begging to escape, but I had made myself a promise—no more crying until this shit was over. I wouldn't give Rain the fucking satisfaction.

Retta, Darcy, and several of the other Blighted men and women who were living here had offered to come fight with us. And while my stomach tightened with worry at the thought, I hadn't tried to talk them out of it. Instead, I'd thanked them gravely and pulled the housekeeper and cook into bone-crushing hugs.

The Blighted who were too infirm to fight would stay behind to watch the kids in the safety of Beatrice's warded house. But although Darcy and Retta were able-bodied, that didn't mean they were fighters. The one reassuring thought I clung to was that enough Gifted and Touched had joined our side that Blighted Resistance members would have solid magical backup.

Only a small group of us would be attempting to break into Rain's mountain stronghold. The rest would distract him by launching an attack on the People's Palace.

The palace was still heavily fortified with guards, but their numbers were lowered. After Rain's coup, some had defected and others had been arrested or killed. Even though the Blighted lacked magic, they would outnumber the guards three or four to one. That should even the odds, or even tip them in our favor.

Retta and I shared a look over her son's head, and I turned away to let her say her goodbyes. He was too young to fully comprehend what was going on, but he knew enough to worry for his mother. I could hear her whispering false reassurances as I walked away.

I rounded the corner into the living room. The TV was off. Ivy kneeled on the couch, resting her elbows on the back of it and taking in the activity around her with wide eyes. A glowing blue portal shimmered on the far wall between two large paintings, courtesy of Jae. My four stood in front of it, talking with the group of Blighted who would accompany us to the Resistance headquarters. From there, we'd split up to undertake our separate missions.

Fen looked up as I approached, reaching out for me. He raised my hand to his lips and nipped at my knuckles. "Ready?"

"Yeah. Will found a few extra transport spells my grandmother had stashed around the house. I swear, these kids know this place better than I ever will."

He chuckled. "I would've loved this house when I was little."

Retta bustled around the corner, using her sleeve to dab at her eyes. "I'm sorry, I'm sorry! I'm ready."

She joined our group, catching Darcy's hand and squeezing it tightly. The kindly, round-faced woman looked grim. I tried to imagine either of them wielding weapons as they stormed the palace, but my brain couldn't conjure up the image.

I tugged Fen aside and gestured our newest recruits through the portal ahead of us. The group of Blighted all walked through, some hesitating slightly as they forced their unwilling bodies to step into the glowing blue light. It was probably the first time they'd been through a portal.

When it was just me and my four left standing by the wall, I turned to them. My gaze moved across their faces, each so different and yet each so strikingly handsome it made my heart ache.

I suddenly didn't know what to say. What were the right words for a moment like this?

"Guys, I…."

My voice faltered, and I swallowed. *Don't cry, godsdamn it.*

165

"We know, Lana. Us too."

Corin smiled, though worry darkened his eyes. He cupped my cheeks and kissed me once, softly, on the lips. I wanted more, so much more, but I knew why he didn't give it to me.

His kiss was a promise. That this wasn't over.

Fen pulled on the hand he was still holding, and I turned toward him. He wrapped his arms around me tightly, and I let myself feel small and safe in his embrace for a moment.

"We got this, killer," he murmured.

A hand cradled the back of my neck, and as Fen released me, Jae spun me around and crashed his lips into mine. I was so surprised I almost lost my balance, and he tightened his grip on me, keeping me upright as he claimed my mouth in a deep, wet kiss.

Akio chuckled, and Fenris wolf-whistled.

When our lips finally broke apart, I was gasping and a little dazed.

Jae smiled at me, his green eyes warm and open. "Just making up for lost time."

I laughed, biting my swollen bottom lip. Then I turned slowly to face Akio. His dark eyes blazed as he stared down at me, and I could feel every moment of our time together yesterday like it was written on my body.

"Thank you for being here with me," I whispered, using those words deliberately. We might be bound together, but I wanted him to have a choice. Always. And I hoped he would always choose me.

Akio dragged a finger down the side of my face, leaving a trail of fire in its wake. "Kitten, there is no one I would rather fight for… or with."

And then there was no more putting it off. We all turned

166

toward the portal, my men falling into a tight group around me. Akio and Corin stepped forward and—

"Wait!"

Ivy's voice made me jump. I'd forgotten she was still here, watching our entire exchange. Gods, we really *were* more entertaining than a TV show.

I shot a glance over my shoulder as she rose from the couch and trotted toward us. "What is it, Ivy?"

"I'm coming with you."

My brow furrowed. "What?"

"I'm coming. To help." Her brown eyes were wide and earnest. "You need extra help, don't you?"

"Well, yeah, but…." I trailed off. Telling her "I thought you just liked to watch" did *not* seem appropriate in this moment.

"I can do that!" Ivy smoothed down her short, lacy flapper dress. "I can't exactly fight like you all, but I can still be useful. I promise!"

"No one doubts that." I hesitated. "But are you sure you want to? It's… human stuff. It doesn't have to be your concern."

A scowl crossed her heart-shaped face. "I don't want to be around forever in the kind of world Rain wants to create."

I shivered involuntarily. *Yeah, I wouldn't either.*

"Right. Of course you can come with us, Ivy. Thank you."

She clapped her delicate hands together, prancing over to the portal. Watching her, I would've thought we were heading to the party of the century instead of a battle against an insane, power-hungry super-mage.

We entered the portal after her, walking quickly through the tunnels and guardroom and entering the Resistance headquarters. The place was buzzing with energy. People hustled through, carrying weapons or other equipment. Wide eyes watched us as we passed, and I tried to look strong and confident instead of slightly nauseated and scared shitless.

When we entered the large common room of the old factory, Corin stiffened.

"Asprix!"

He broke away from our group, striding toward the little alcove off to one side of the room where the old reader, Asprix, could usually be found.

But not today.

Today, he was standing in the common area, clutching a long staff as a younger Resistance member strapped pieces of what looked like makeshift leather armor to him.

"Asprix! What are you doing?"

Corin's voice was tense, and we all changed course to trail after him as he neared the old man.

"Oh, dear boy! I hoped I would see you before the fight began." Asprix's face lit as he looked up at Corin.

My heart twinged. I hadn't realized how small Asprix was. He'd always been sitting when we came to visit, and next to Corin's tall, muscled form, he looked tiny—like he might blow away in a strong wind.

"The fight?" Corin's face darkened. "I hope you don't mean you're joining the attack."

The boy assisting Asprix finished tying a final knot and darted away, shooting a wide-eyed glance back at us. The old man grabbed onto his staff with both hands, drawing himself up another inch, although his back refused to straighten fully. "Of course I am, dear boy. I must."

"*No*. No, you don't have to do that. You can't."

Asprix's kindly face relaxed, his wrinkles deepening as he smiled. "I *can't?* Well then, why can he?" He gestured with his chin

168

to a Resistance member passing by. "Why can she?" He jerked his chin the other way, toward a woman sharpening a small dagger. "Why can any of them? And I can't?" A sweep of his head encompassed the entire room.

"Be... because—"

"Because you'll worry about me?" He raised a gnarled hand to Corin's cheek. "My dear boy, thank you for caring. But someone else could say the same about any person here. Should we *all* not fight, because our loved ones don't want to lose us? What then? Who wins then?"

"I don't..." Corin shook his head.

Stepping up beside him, I laid a hand on his arm and squeezed gently.

"Corin. Remember how much you wanted to fight? How badly you wish you could have?" I didn't say more than that, but I knew his thoughts went immediately to his family and the Gifted mob that had attacked them. The muscles of his arm bunched under my fingertips.

Cursing softly, Corin pulled Asprix into a tight but careful hug. "Come back alive, old man. I mean it."

"Oh, I fully intend to, dear boy." The reader patted Corin gently on the back.

"There you all are!"

Noble strode toward us quickly. He was dressed for battle too, with thick leather boots, cargo pants, and a dark, long-sleeved shirt. A leather vest covered his torso. It would offer little protection against the kinds of magical firepower he'd likely be up against, but it was better than nothing. The young girl, whose name I'd learned was Serena, kept pace a step behind him. She wore the same look of fierce determination she had last time I'd seen her.

"Are you ready for this?" the Resistance leader murmured, coming to stand beside me.

"Fuck no."

He barked a laugh. "That's a very sane answer."

"How are things here?" My gaze darted around the large space.

"We're as prepared as we can be for so many unknowns. We need to get moving though. Everyone's energy is peaking, and if we don't give them something to fight soon, it'll flip over into nerves."

My fingers reached down to caress the twin blades strapped to my thighs. I may have magic at my disposal now, but I wasn't about to leave them behind.

"Then let's do this."

"Ha! No time for bullshit. I knew I liked you, Crow." Noble shot me a smile then jerked his head for me to follow him.

My four followed behind us as Noble led me to a small raised platform near the entrance to the room. He stepped up onto it, bringing me with him. As he did, the hubbub of voices in the large space died down immediately. I blinked. He hadn't even used magic.

I stared out at a sea of faces and saw hope, fear, and interest reflected back at me. An elbow dug into my ribs, and I shot a glance at Noble.

"Talk to them," he murmured, nudging me forward a step.

Ah, fuck. Couldn't we just skip this part and go right to the life-threatening danger?

I licked my lips, drawing in a breath. I didn't know the spell to amplify my voice, but Jae caught my eye and nodded. Apparently, he did.

"I used to hate the Gifted."

My voice rang out across the room, filling the space.

Absolute silence fell, and I swallowed thickly before continuing.

"I hated the Touched too, I guess. With good reason. I grew up in a Blighted settlement, and I knew magic users who did nothing but abuse their power and exploit others. But the thing was…" I paused, looking down at my four, who were gathered in front of the platform, Ivy beside them. "The thing was, I didn't know *all* magic users, or even most of them. I didn't know some of them could be good, honorable, and brave. I divided people into simple groups, and I didn't look beyond that. But I'm learning, slowly, to consider people as individuals rather than defining them by their group. To trust people who give me a reason to—whether they're Gifted, Touched, or Blighted."

My voice gained strength as I continued.

"I would never tell you to forget the past. I wouldn't even ask you to forgive. But I ask you to look around at the people gathered in this room and realize that we're all on the same side today."

Looking at the faces before me, I tried to memorize each one. Some of them might not be with us tomorrow, and I wanted to honor their presence here today.

"I have chosen to trust the people who give me reason to, and you've all given me very good reason. This fight isn't about letting go of the past; it's about building the future we want. The future we all deserve. Maybe once we've fought together, even faced death together—maybe out of the darkness of this moment, a better future can rise."

My magically amplified words echoed slightly and died out.

No one spoke.

Then a man midway to the back raised his hands, holding

them over his head in the shape of a crow. The gesture spread across the room until I stared out at a sea of hands and fingers splayed like wings.

The weight of their faith in me made my heart thump desperately in my chest, but I didn't back away from it this time. I raised my own hands, mirroring their gesture. Then we all brought our hands down together, almost like a salute.

Noble clapped me on the shoulder, flashing me a smile that would've been smug if he hadn't looked so proud. He turned to address the crowd, his voice magically amplified like mine had been.

"This is it, everyone. We're as ready as we can be. We've gone over our plans and outfitted ourselves as best we can. We've set our course of action. Now there's only one thing left to do—bring down that bastard, Rain. It's time to show him that many people working together are stronger than even the most powerful mage in the world." He raised his fist in the air, his voice rising to match it. "Time to make him pay for his crimes against all of us. To turn the tide of evil in the world. 'To reap the harvest of perpetual peace, by this one bloody trial of sharp war!'"

The room exploded into noise as a battle cry went up among the gathered crowd. They stomped their feet and banged their weapons, their voices uniting into a single roar.

I shot a glance at Noble, my words barely audible above the crowd. "*Richard III*, huh? You read it?"

He grinned at me, his eyes flashing. "Well, when The Crow quotes Shakespeare to you, you damn well better quote it back. And besides," he added, his smile widening to show his teeth. "Richmond wins in the end."

CHAPTER 21

THE SCENT of pine and earth filled my nostrils, and I lowered my nose to the ground, searching for any sign of Rain or his minions.

There was none, but I knew we were on the right path. I could pick up the lingering scent of my four, and even myself, from our trek down the mountainside after I escaped Rain's compound.

Ugh, I really did smell like I'd spent a week in a dungeon. Why didn't you tell me?

Fen sniffed at the trail beside me. *I didn't notice. All I could focus on was that you were alive.*

I snorted internally. That had to be a lie. But there was no hint of anything but truth in the thoughts and feelings coming from him.

My gaze caught his in the darkness, the amber eyes of his wolf lighter than his usual chocolate brown. *Gods, you really must love me.*

The wave of emotion pouring off him nearly bowled me over, and he licked the side of my face. *Don't ever doubt it, killer.*

"No making out on missions," Corin murmured beside me. His body brushed against mine, keeping in close contact as Fen and I led our small team up the mountain.

"That's a terrible rule," Akio drawled from Fen's other side.

"Of course you would say that," Corin deadpanned, though he didn't argue Akio's point.

The clear night sky was painted with stars, and a half-moon gave us enough light to see by. Ivy's ghostly form was almost invisible as she walked a few feet away from me. Emil and Foster, the two Gifted men who could break wards, brought up the rear of our party. Once they let us inside Rain's compound, they'd rejoin the others and give Noble the signal to launch the attack.

We'd arrived at the base of the mountain through a portal created by another new Gifted recruit. She'd closed it after us to protect those who had remained behind—children and others too old or sick to fight. A small team of able-bodied Resistance members had stayed to protect them, but nearly everyone was joining the fight.

A few similar portals had been opened a short distance from the People's Palace. We had a limited supply of transport spells, and it was better to use them as a way out than as a way in.

The placement of the portal at the mountain's base was deliberate. We could've had it deliver us right to Rain's doorstep, but hiking in gave us an element of surprise and allowed us to scope out the area first. While the attack on the palace would be blatant and violent, the whole point of our mission was to stay under the radar.

A new smell hit my nose, and I stopped suddenly, hackles rising as my skin prickled. *Do you smell that?*

Rain. Fen's hatred of the man infused the word. *And a few others. I don't know all the scents, but Jonas Nocturne was here, for sure.*

I smell Nicholas Constantine. Victor Kruger, too. And... Eben Knowles.

Shit. Fen growled. *Rain must've brought him in this way.*

Gaze fixed ahead of us on the dark pines and undergrowth, I padded forward slowly. Corin's hand was buried in my fur as he crept along beside me.

"There," Jae murmured from just behind me.

Several yards in front of us, a large slab of rock rose tall, creating a sheer cliff face. Tucked away in the crook where the rock met the steep mountainside sat the small, hidden entrance to Rain's compound. It hadn't been warded last time I'd seen it, but now a soft purple light pulsed across the surface.

I shifted back to human form quickly, pleased I didn't lose a single article of clothing in the transformation. Fen shifted next to me, and we all gathered into a small huddle.

"This is the door we came through when I escaped," I whispered softly. "There's an inner door several yards inside the tunnel that's warded too. Emil, Foster—can you break both of them?"

The two men nodded in unison and got to work on the first door.

Ivy stepped up to my side. "Want me to look inside?"

"Yeah. Find out if there are any guards at the doors. But don't let them see you."

She smiled happily. "Of course I won't, silly!"

Then she stepped into the rock face next to the door, disappearing from view.

The rest of us fanned out around the entrance as the two men worked, our gazes darting up and down the mountainside. The quiet stillness of the night seemed threatening somehow, and every animal call or rustle of wind through the pines set my teeth on edge.

After what felt like an eternity, Ivy popped back out of the rock, her wide eyes finding me in the dark. "No guards behind the first door. Three behind the second. A mage, a demon, and a tiger shifter."

I nodded, turning to Emil and Foster. "Did you get that?"

Foster nodded, the sheen of sweat on his brow gleaming in the moonlight. The ward brightened briefly then flickered out of existence, leaving behind a smell like burning hair.

The door wasn't locked. Rain believed too strongly in the power of magic to stoop to anything as mundane as a lock to keep intruders out.

Summoning my magic, I created a small ball of light in the palm of my hand then sent it up to hover above us. I'd asked Jae to teach me the spell this morning and was pleased at how quickly I had picked it up.

It was useful as fuck on missions like this.

Jae and I led Emil, Foster, and Ivy through the dimly lit tunnel in silence. When the inner door came into view, I tamped down the glow of my light even more and gestured the two Gifted men ahead of me.

They got to work silently, trading small pulses of magic that weakened the glowing ward. When it finally flared and died, I braced myself, half expecting the door to burst open and the guards to come charging through.

But they didn't.

"Ivy," I breathed. "Look inside again. Only this time, *do* let them see you."

Her eyes widened, and she nodded excitedly. She stepped into the rock wall beside us. A moment later, a shout of surprise sounded from the other side of the door.

With a nod to Jae, I yanked the door open, revealing the three guards on the other side. They were turned away from us as they watched Ivy prance down the corridor. She'd made herself more corporeal, though she was still slightly translucent.

Not giving them a chance to react, I hurled both daggers in quick succession at the red-skinned demon on the right, hitting him in the back. He gurgled and keeled over. The other two turned toward us just as Jae sent an ice spear through the mage's chest and I unleashed a ball of flame that engulfed the tiger. A loud, animal cry shredded the silence, and I quickly pulled back on the magic.

Jae sent out a flaming arc that opened up the tiger's throat. Blood poured from the wound, and the cry died out as the shifter slumped to the ground.

"Fuck," I muttered. "That could've been quieter."

"You did well," Jae reassured me. "We ended it quickly, at least."

Fear chilled my skin, but I didn't hear any other sounds coming down the hallway. Maybe backup wasn't close by enough to have heard the noise.

I turned back to Emil and Foster, who looked slightly shell-shocked. They'd probably never been up close and personal to a fight like this in their lives. I hoped they were fast learners. "Thanks, guys. We'll take it from here."

Emil nodded, tugging a transport spell from his pocket. He dropped it, clapped a hand on Foster's shoulder, and crushed the glass with his heel.

As the smoke billowed out, enveloping them in a purple cloud, I activated my communication charm.

"Noble? We're in. We're sending Emil and Foster back to you. Good luck."

His voice sounded in my ear immediately. "You too. Keep your communication charm on. We'll be in touch."

The earrings enchanted with a communication charm dangled from my ears, at odds with the rest of my tactical outfit. I was dressed in black, with my dagger sheaths strapped to my thighs and thick, heavy boots on my feet.

Ivy had drifted back out of the tunnel to collect the rest of my four, and they joined us after a moment. Going from memory, I retraced the path I'd taken during my escape, passing by the hallway where I'd found my men. Jae's hand brushed my arm as we walked by it, and he smiled lightly.

After a few more twists and turns, the tunnel opened up into the large room where Rain stored the concentrated ball of magic from his first pull—the one that had caused the Great Death.

I slowed as we entered the room, worry twisting like a snake in my gut.

Wall sconces glowing with magic illuminated the large space, but they were the only source of light left.

The ball of magic that had burned as brightly and powerfully as a star was gone. So was the large metal platform with the six huge prongs that had held the magic like a gem. The large space was barren, the emptiness all the more striking because of what the room had once contained.

"It's gone," I breathed, a chill skittering down my spine.

"What's gone?" Corin glanced back at me before continuing his perusal of the huge space.

"The magic." Lingering traces of the power that had once been kept here remained, raising the hairs on the back of my neck. But I couldn't feel anything more than that. "This was where Rain kept the magic he stole. What the hell did he do with it? He told me he couldn't access it. Shit. Do you think he found a way?"

"If he did, the Resistance attack will be over before it begins," Jae said, his voice hard. "He could make himself so powerful we'd never be able to defeat him. He'd be able to wipe us out with a flick of his finger."

I swallowed. "Maybe that's why there are so few guards down here. He doesn't think he needs them."

"Well, no matter how much power he has, there's only one way to stop him from getting more." Fen bared his teeth, the expression wolf-like even in his human form. "Find that fucking machine and destroy it."

Ivy was already walking up the stairs at the perimeter of the room to the second level. We hustled after her, careful to keep our footsteps quiet. I'd expected this place to be crawling with guards, and the eerie emptiness was making me nervous. Maybe our plan really *was* working, and Rain had called in all the manpower he could spare to help defend the palace.

We turned into a hallway leading away from the second floor of the large room. I stepped to the front of the group, my hands raised and at the ready. I'd passed through the protection spells on these tunnels before, so I knew better than the others what to expect.

Two yards in, the tunnel shook slightly as a piece of rock pulled itself away from the wall, forming a roughly human shape.

"Shit. Here we go."

I threw a strong gust of wind at the stone figure, driving it back down the tunnel. It hurled a piece of itself at me, a large chunk of rock the size of my head. I blasted the flying boulder with a shot of flame, and it exploded. I winced at the noise—I hadn't learned yet how to fight quietly with magic. Jae stepped up beside me, raising a hand toward the creature.

It thundered down the tunnel toward us, but as it ran, its body seemed to vibrate. When its next heavy footfall hit the earth, cracks streaked up its leg, and before it took two more steps, its entire body crumbled into a pile of rocks.

Scrambling over the chunks of stone, I shot a glance back at Jae. "I like your way better than mine."

"I'll teach you how to do it someday. Earth is a difficult element to master, but I know you're up to the challenge."

Everyone else clambered over the rock pile obstructing the hallway—except Ivy, who walked right through it. I kept my eyes on the walls, searching for the telltale vibration that would signal the arrival of another rock creature.

The sconces on the walls cast a yellow light through the tunnel, fading almost to black in the space between the magical lights. I turned left. We were close to the dungeon where I'd been kept, if my memory was accurate.

I glanced back over my shoulder to tell the men that, but the words died in my throat. From several yards away, a fireball hurtled through the tunnel toward us.

CHAPTER 22

"Lana!"

Corin's shout drew my attention, and I whirled around.

An arc of blue flame bore down on us from the other direction, boxing us in.

I didn't think. I just summoned the biggest tornado of air I could. It sprang to life around me and my four, tearing at the walls and ceiling of the crude rock tunnel. The twin orange and blue flames collided with it, whipping around us in a funnel of heat and smoke. The wind pressed in on us, forced closer by the flames even as it extinguished them.

Finally, the fireballs died out. I let the wind fall away, my ears still ringing from its loud howl.

Our attackers had been invisible, but now that they no longer had the element of surprise, they slowly faded into view. Advancing on us from each end of the long hallway were two groups of guards—Gifted and Touched, it looked like. The front lines were packed tightly together in the tunnel, and I could see their backup close behind them.

"Shit."

The word had barely escaped my mouth when both groups attacked us again. A fireball hurtled through the tunnel from one direction, while several ice spears flew from the other side.

"Watch out!" Fire met fire as I hurled an orange ball of flame toward the incoming attack.

Jae threw up a wall of ice on our other side, blocking the spears. Another blast of fire from our attackers hit his ice blockade. Water poured off it as it cracked and began to melt, pooling on the uneven floor and making the ground slippery.

A moment later, a gray-skinned demon slammed into it like a battering ram. The ice wall disintegrated, and he didn't hesitate. He sprang toward Corin, moving at lightning speed. His hands landed around Corin's neck, but Akio leapt on the demon from behind, cutting his throat cleanly.

Corin dodged the spray of blood then looked up at the incubus. "Thanks."

"Anytime." Akio grinned.

Another ball of fire flew toward us from the opposite end of the tunnel. This time, I forced an enormous gust of wind through the tunnel, turning the fire back on itself and making the guards at the end of hallway stumble back. Baring my teeth, I pushed the magic harder; the wind picked up speed and screamed through the small space as it drove our attackers backward.

"Ivy!" I called over the shrieking of the wind. "Go ahead of us! See if you can find Rain's magic pulling machine. It's the device he uses to run his spell. We need to destroy it!"

"On it!" she cried, her musical voice fierce. She plunged through the wall to my right.

Behind me, grunts and cries echoed as my four dealt with the attackers from that end of the tunnel. I heard them calling warnings and instructions as they fought, and I was suddenly grateful they'd been a team for so long. They functioned as a cohesive unit, moving in tandem and always looking out for each other.

"We've got an opening!" Fen shouted. "Lana!"

My hands shook from the effort of sustaining the wind. Abruptly, I pulled back on the magic then unleashed a large ball of fire down the hallway before the guards could recover.

I turned to my four, chest heaving. "Go!"

We raced down the hallway, Akio in the lead. The guards behind us weren't all dead, but it would take them a moment to recover from the wind and fire. That was enough for us to solidify our lead.

When we rounded a corner, I caught a flash of someone disappearing through an archway at the end of the hall. Dark hair whipped around her head as she glanced back at me.

Kate.

"Rain's disciple! She'll know where the magic pull is." I pointed. "We need to catch her!"

"You two go." Jae jerked his head toward Akio and me. "We'll hold off the guards."

Akio's gaze caught mine, and we sprinted forward. The room at the end of the hall was familiar. I'd spent days staring out at the large open space surrounded by cells when I'd been locked in one of them myself.

By the time we burst through the archway, Kate had nearly reached the other tunnel that connected to this room on the opposite side.

With an inarticulate shout, I reached out with my magic and

183

plucked her from the ground, lifting her several feet in the air. She twisted, throwing a hand over her shoulder to shoot a bolt of lightning at me. Akio and I dove to the side, avoiding the strike.

Borrowing a page from Jonas's playbook, I slammed Kate against the ground before raising her high again. It was a dirty fucking move, but I wanted to win this fight. I'd worry about playing fair later.

She moved to throw another bolt of electricity at us, but I dropped her against the rough stone floor again. I left her there this time, diving on top of her and pinning her body down with my own.

Kate pressed up to her hands and knees, trying to shake me off. I clung tightly, slipping an arm around her neck in a chokehold. The sounds of a fight filtered in from the hallway behind us, but I had to assume Jae, Corin, and Fen were safe. They could handle themselves.

"Akio!" I called, but he was way ahead of me.

He crouched down beside us, murmuring into Kate's ear. I couldn't hear exactly what he was saying, but the deep timbre of his voice sent shivers racing through me.

Kate leaned toward him, seeming to forget all about my hold on her. His lips found her ear, whispering promises of sinfully sweet pleasure. A moan worked its way out of her mouth, and I scrambled off her, wiping my hands on my pants. I felt dirty all of a sudden.

Though I tried not to watch as Akio pulled Kate slowly to her feet, I couldn't tear my gaze away. Unreasonable jealousy burned in my stomach, but I forced it down.

He was using her. He would never use me. When he whispered promises into my ear, he meant them.

Akio's large hand tipped her face up, his dark eyes blazing as he looked down at her. "Kate. Where does Rain keep the machine for his magic pull? What did he do with the magic he already stole?"

She licked her lips greedily, pushing against his grip to try to bring her face closer to his, but he kept her still. Her eyes burning with desire, she murmured softly, "On the upper level, near the peak of the mountain. He moved the old magic there too. He'll try to access it again after he does his second pull."

"How do we turn the machine off? How do we stop it?"

Kate smiled seductively at him. "You can't. He's the only one who can use it."

He shot a glance at me over her head. "We'll have to break it then."

"He'll stop you." Kate laughed, a throaty sound. "He's destined to be the most powerful mage in the world. And I'll be right there by his side."

The look Akio shot her was full of disgust, though she probably couldn't see that through the haze of his charm.

"Lock yourself in one of those cells," he instructed, his voice hard. "Forget you saw us. And forget you ever knew Rain. Forget it all."

Her gaze lost focus, and she stumbled away from him, weaving across the room like a drunk at last call. She unlocked the door of one of the small cells then dropped the keys to the ground and stepped inside. I hurried over, retrieved the key ring, and locked her in.

She watched me dazedly, the usual malicious glint in her dark eyes gone.

I looked back at Akio. "Will she really forget she knows Rain?"

He shrugged, coming to stand next to me. "Probably not. But I had to try."

As he neared, Kate licked her lips. She reached through the small window toward him, grimacing in pain as her arm touched the metal bars. Her fingertips brushed against his chest, and I slapped her hand away. We'd already gotten all the useful information we could out of her, and I was sick of watching her try to grope my man.

Her arm slithered back through the window, and Akio raised an eyebrow at me. "Jealous, kitten?"

"What?" I scoffed, a flush rising in my cheeks. "No."

He backed me up against the wall next to the door. "I like you jealous. I like to see your claws out. But you don't need them now. Because now that I've had you, I'm never letting you go. Yours are the only legs I want wrapped around me."

Heat ran through me as he dropped his lips to mine, claiming my mouth in a possessive kiss.

"Oh, for fuck's sake! I thought we said no making out on missions."

I jumped as Fenris darted into the room, followed closely by Jae and Corin. I slipped out from between Akio and the wall, hurrying over to join them.

"I never agreed to that," the incubus drawled.

"Well, while you two were getting cozy, some of us were busy holding off a shitload of guards. The ones who attacked us in the hall are dead, but more have to be coming. We weren't quiet about it." Fen grabbed my hand, pulling me toward the tunnel on the far end of the room. "We gotta move!"

"Did you find out anything useful?" Corin asked as we ran, keeping pace with Akio behind me.

"Yeah. Kate told us where the machine for the magic pull is.

We need to get to it before Rain comes back." I pressed the communication charm at my ear. "Noble? You there?"

"I'm here."

Sounds of a fight in the background accompanied his voice, and my stomach clenched. The people attacking the palace were giving us a chance to find and destroy Rain's magic pull by keeping him occupied. We couldn't let this chance slip away.

"We've got a lead on the machine. How are things going on your end?"

"All right. The palace was more heavily fortified than we expected, but with the help of the Gifted Resistance members, we were able to breach several weak points. And we've got numbers on our side."

I tugged Fen's arm, leading him down an offshoot hallway. "Good. There are quite a few guards here too, but so far we've been able to get past them. Have you seen Rain?"

"Yeah." Noble's words came in between sharp breaths, like he was running too. "He hurled bolts of lightning from the top floor of the palace when we breached the entrance. We're working our way up. We've taken out most of the guards."

The tunnel we were in opened up into a large space—what looked like a natural cave in the rock repurposed as a huge storage room. Magical lights shone down from high ceilings, and two sets of stairways were carved along the walls, leading to doors high above. Several large hunks of metal and broken pieces of machinery littered the floor.

Jerking my head toward one of the staircases, I made a beeline for it. Kate had said the magic pulling machine was on the highest level.

"Well, keep him distracted, and let me know if you see him

again. We'll destroy his machine soon and join you at the palace as soon as we—"

My words cut off as a large puff of purple smoke exploded into the middle of the room. Rain stepped out of the haze, followed closely by Jonas, Victor, and Nicholas. Several other Gifted and Touched goons stood behind them.

"Never mind." My voice was thick. "We found him."

CHAPTER 23

"Is he there? Lana? Shit! Are you all right?"

Noble's voice echoed in my ear, but the words hardly registered.

I stood stock-still, staring at Rain. His mousy brown hair with streaks of gray at the temples, the bags under his eyes, the small gap between his front teeth—they all made him look so human, so *normal*.

But the veneer of civility and sanity was slowly chipping away. There was a mad glint in his eyes I hadn't noticed before, a harshness to the set of his mouth.

"I should have known you'd leave your friends to fight and come here, Miss Lockwood. I see you had a little chat with Kate." He stepped forward, and his lackeys mirrored his movement. "You've never been able to just step back and let things play their course. You always have to interfere. Just like your father."

My heart thudded hard, my blood rushing so fast I thought my veins would burst. "I *am* like my father. Except this time, I'm actually going to stop you."

He smiled, and tension filled the space. "Don't you imagine that's what he thought too? That he would succeed in stopping me? But even then, I couldn't be held back. Now? There's nothing that can stop me."

As he spoke, he gestured with both hands. Bright bolts of lightning flew from his palms, twining together and driving toward me. I threw out a fireball, but the bolt barely slowed down. It absorbed the fire and barreled toward me, and I used the half-second of time I'd gained to throw myself out of the way.

The lightning slammed into the wall with a boom, sending sparks flying in all directions. The hair on my arms stood straight up, and my whole body thrummed from the electric charge in the air.

Holy fuck.

He'd gotten even stronger.

I leapt to my feet, my legs shaking beneath me, and hurled the biggest fireball I could conjure in Rain's direction. It felt paltry compared to the blast he'd just unleashed, and he didn't even bother to block it. He just swept his hand to the side and the fireball changed direction, hitting the wall harmlessly.

"If that's the best you can do, you *are* in trouble, Miss Lockwood." The Gifted man smiled ominously.

"And look, she brought her Blighted pet to this fight." Nicholas's lip curled in smug disgust. "I'll take that one."

Fear and rage exploded in my chest. It was one thing for Rain to threaten me, but the look in Nicholas's eyes as he glared at Corin made my skin crawl.

Electric magic crackled between Nicholas's fingertips, and he stepped forward.

I moved to intercept him, but before I could, all hell broke loose.

Apparently deciding the time for making grandiose speeches was past, all four of the Gifted men before us attacked at once. Nicholas's bolt charged toward Corin, who dove out of the way. Jonas hurled a fireball toward Fenris, and Victor lashed out at Akio with a whip made of white light, catching his forearm with the stinging tail.

Rain threw what looked like a web of lightning toward us—it expanded as it flew through the air, wide enough to strike us all.

"Water!" I screamed to Jae, pushing the magic out of myself with the force of a tsunami. He joined my effort, and a wave of water crashed toward the electric web. They met with an ear-splitting popping sound, and the web exploded. The water flashed with light before splashing to the floor. It ran in a torrent over the uneven floor, pooling in one corner of the room.

At least we had an effective defense against the lightning magic.

Water splashed the Representatives as it struck the earth, but Rain didn't look any less terrifying soaking wet. In fact, he looked madder and meaner.

His chest heaved with angry breaths, and he gestured again. All the rocks and stones littering the ground, large and small, rose into the air.

Oh shit.

He flung his arms forward, and the stones hurtled toward us, impossibly fast. I barely had time to turn away before they reached us. Small stones bit into my skin like snakebites, and a large rock struck me between the shoulder blades, throwing me forward. I slid on the wet ground, scraping my palms and knees as the breath left my lungs.

I coughed and heard someone groan beside me.

Oh, gods, no. This could not be how this ended. I refused to go up against a super-mage and get killed by a bunch of fucking rocks.

Stumbling to my feet, I turned around, reaching out with my magic and latching onto Rain. He began to rise into the air, propelled by my levitation spell. His face contorted with surprise, and his body jerked.

"Get them! I'll handle her."

At his barked command, the other Representatives and their backup raced toward us. The sounds of shouts and explosions reverberated through the room, but I kept my focus on Rain. I had to trust that my men would take care of each other. And if I killed Rain, I could end all of this.

He was almost twenty feet in the air now, and he raised his hands to attack. Switching directions, I used my magic to propel him toward the earth. He flew downward, but when he was several inches from the floor of the cave he... stopped. His magic pressed back against mine, arresting his movement.

I broke away with a gasp, unable to sustain the spell against his power. He righted himself, landing gently on his feet.

"You're resourceful. I'll give you that." Rain dipped his head mockingly. "But let me show you how it's really done."

He threw both hands out, and a jet of wind hit me like a punch to the solar plexus. It picked me up and drove me across the room, slamming me into the wall so hard I felt like I'd been hit by a speeding car. It pinned me there, the force so strong I couldn't even raise my arms.

All I could do was watch in horror as Rain advanced toward me through the battlefield.

Several yards away, Jonas threw blast after blast of flame at Jae. I knew Jae was good, but his father was the one who had taught him to fight, and Jonas was using every bit of that advantage now. Fen and Corin tried to hold off Nicholas, who attacked wildly. And Akio was doing his best against Victor Kruger's magical whips, but I saw several more gashes on his arms and torso.

We were strong, but Rain was winning.

The thought made my blood boil, and I renewed my struggles against the wind pressing me back. The pressure was so intense it stole the breath from my lungs and made my eyes water.

When Rain was a few feet from me, he raised a hand. A huge sword made of fire appeared in his grip, it's hilt a shiny dark metal. The wind finally released me, and I fell to the floor, sucking in ragged breaths of air. The sharp toe of his dress shoe dug into my stomach as he kicked me. When I rolled over, his foot slammed into my chest, holding me down while he raised the flaming sword above me.

Before he could land a killing blow, dozens of small green balls of light surrounded him. They moved in unison, knocking Rain off his feet. The sword vanished as he toppled.

I blinked. Who the hell had done that? Jae? I'd never seen him use magic like that before.

The little balls of power were pressing against Rain's attempts to rise. I scrambled up, glancing around the room. My jaw dropped.

Olene? And Noble!

The Resistance leader had joined Akio against Victor, and several other Resistance members fanned out behind them to fight the guards. But I couldn't take my eyes off Olene. She strode forward, her hands whipping through the air in front of her, and as they did, the balls of light surrounding Rain moved at her command, beating against his body and keeping him off balance.

He crossed his arms over his chest, and a web of lightning

surrounded his body. There was a pulse of electricity and the balls of power exploded outward. Olene fell back a step, but in a heartbeat she was on Rain again.

"Help your friends. I'll hold him off!" Using the small green orbs as a battering ram, she drove Rain backward.

She didn't have to tell me twice. I wasn't sure what she was doing here, or why she had arrived with Noble. But with the extra firepower on our side, we actually had a chance.

I spun around, rushing back into the fray.

Corin's shirt was singed, and Fen's fur seemed to stand on end as they fought against Nicholas. The Gifted man threw bolt after bolt of lightning their way, keeping them on the defensive.

"*Hey!*" My voice cut across the noise of battle, and Nicholas's head jerked my way.

Corin looked too, and as I ran, I flashed him our gesture for *distraction* and pointed to myself. His brow furrowed, and then he nodded. I hurled a ball of fire at Nicholas, forcing him to turn to deal with me. He blocked it with a bolt of white light, and I switched up my attack, throwing an ice spear at him.

His lightning exploded the ice with a crackling sound, and he cackled wildly. He was too busy laughing to notice Corin running up behind him. Corin leapt onto his back, sliding an arm around his throat and reaching around to shove a small vial into his mouth. Then he shoved his chin up, clamping his jaw shut.

The greasy-haired man choked and sputtered as I raced toward him, raising his hands to electrocute Corin. Before he could make contact, I launched myself into the air, using all of my forward momentum to land a punch on Nicholas's face.

I felt his jaw break, along with the glass vial inside his mouth. His half-lidded eyes opened wide as iridescent black liquid dribbled down his chin. Nicholas's mouth opened in an approximation of a scream, but nothing came out except black bubbles and a gurgling sound.

He fell to his knees, hands scrabbling at his throat, lightning spurting in small, weak bursts from his fingertips. Then he toppled over.

Corin's eyes flashed with triumph and disgust as he gazed down at Nicholas. But they softened when they turned to me. "Thanks for having my back."

I grinned fiercely. "Always."

We didn't have time to relish our victory though. A howl caught my attention, and I whirled around. Fenris, still in wolf form, was facing down several guards. More were appearing through the same door we'd entered from. Rain must've called for extra reinforcements.

Corin and I raced toward Fen.

"How many more potions do you have?" I called.

"Five!"

"Then we'd better make 'em count!"

We surged into the thick of the fight. I threw balls of fire, followed in quick succession by my daggers. The change from magic to nonmagical attacks put the guards off balance, and I managed to take two out quickly.

A particularly vicious elementalist drove me backward, using his fire to separate me from the others. I fought back with water, finally managing to bowl him over with a strong blast. His head struck the ground and his eyes rolled back. I leapt forward to deliver a finishing blow when movement in my periphery caught my attention.

It was Ivy.

The ghost raced toward me, heedless of the battle going on around—and sometimes through—her.

"Lana! Lana, come quick! I have to show you something."

"Kinda busy right now, Ivy," I panted, gesturing at the chaos around me.

A body lay a few feet from me. A woman. Blonde hair partially covered a face with delicate features.

My heart rising in my throat, I dashed over, smoothing the hair back to reveal Olene's pale complexion. I felt for a pulse and found a weak but steady thrum. But if she had been fighting Rain....

I scanned the room, searching for the lanky mage's brown and silver hair.

He was nowhere to be found.

"Shit. Where the hell is Rain?" I whispered.

Ivy crouched down beside me, her flapper dress and blonde bob looking out of place in this dingy cave. "That's what I have to show you. I found the magic pulling machine. And Rain is turning it on."

CHAPTER 24

Fear iced my skin.

"What?"

"He's trying to do the pull now. It's up there." She pointed to the door at the top of one of the staircases along the wall. A glowing blue light emanated from the corridor beyond it.

"Show me," I urged, scrambling to my feet. The fight still raged around me, but the noise of it seemed to dim as my focus narrowed. It was too soon for him to do the magic pull, wasn't it? I thought the spell needed longer to recharge.

Ivy nodded fervently then rose and ran toward the staircase. I was a bit slower than her, since I actually had to dodge moving bodies and projectiles instead of passing right through them. She trotted quickly up the stairs, although her feet never actually touched the steps. I took them two at a time after her, my lungs burning and my body aching with exhaustion.

I'd never used this much magic all at once before, and I hadn't realized what a physical toll it would take. I felt like I'd just run up a mountain while being pelted with rocks.

Actually, that was a fairly accurate description of my night so far.

At the top of the stairs, Ivy turned into a long corridor. It was illuminated by glowing blue lights, and it wound around in a tight spiral, moving upward at a steep angle. As I ran, I reached for the communication charm on my earring. I needed to tell Noble and the others where I was—where *Rain* was.

But my hand closed around bare earlobe. I cursed. The fucking earring must've fallen off when Rain pinned me to the wall with wind. My footsteps slowed as I fought an internal war with myself. I wanted to go back, to tell someone what was happening, but I wasn't sure I could spare the precious seconds.

Mind made up, I put on a burst of speed, sprinting after Ivy.

I had to stop Rain.

Careful not to trip, I brought my focus inward, mentally erasing the image of myself. It was entirely possible Rain had a charm like most of the guards at the People's Palace wore that would allow him to see through an invisibility spell. But it was worth trying, at least.

"Ivy!" I hissed, my breath coming in sharp gasps. "Can you make yourself less visible?"

She turned back to me, her eyes finding mine immediately. Apparently, ghosts weren't fooled by invisibility spells.

"Oh, yes!" A few seconds later, she faded from view almost entirely. I could see an outline of her form if I looked closely, but it was nearly indistinguishable. "How's this?"

"Good," I muttered. "Just stick close to me so I don't lose you, okay?"

"I will." A shiver of cold raced up my arm as she brushed against me.

Finally, the corridor leveled out, and a door appeared at the end of it. It stood slightly ajar, just wide enough that if I exhaled all the air from my lungs, I could slip through without touching it.

Ivy passed right through the wood, and a moment later, her face flickered into view through the crack. "He's distracted. Quick! Follow me."

Her voice was so low I had to strain to hear it. Making my body as thin as possible, I slid through the opening in the door. Another cold brush of her hand pulled my attention, and she led me toward a stout pillar at the side of the room. I ducked behind it, peering out slowly into the large space.

Rain moved quickly around the room, flipping switches and sending small jolts of electricity into parts of his machine. Jonas stood to one side, watching anxiously.

The room was big, though nowhere near as cavernous as the space below us where the battle still raged. It had a high, domed ceiling with a small hole in the center. The night sky and stars were visible outside. We must be near the mountain's peak.

I didn't linger on that thought, because my attention was immediately taken up by the contents of the room. Set along one wall, the metal platform with the prongs sticking out of it held the magic from Rain's first pull. The dense ball of power glowed, pulsing with energy.

A large device dominated the center of the room. Rain's magic pulling machine was simple and almost beautiful, comprised of a shining metal platform topped by curved pieces of metal. The pieces created an orb, which was suspended by a thick arm that arced up from the base. A small ball of light glowed inside the orb.

Several feet away from the contraption, a figure sat slumped and still in a chair.

Eben Knowles.

His dark skin was ashen, and though his eyes were open, he didn't seem to be truly seeing anything. A thin ribbon of drool slid from the corner of his mouth.

Pity and revulsion roiled my stomach at the sight of him. If this was what Rain's new machine did to its victims, death might be a better option.

I almost jumped when Rain himself stepped forward and hauled Eben from the chair. He tossed the once-Gifted man aside, and Eben gave no resistance. When he hit the floor, he crawled dazedly away. Rain kicked away the chair Eben had been sitting in. His movements were forceful and jerky, and I couldn't tell if it was from adrenaline or fear or the massive amounts of power surging through his body.

Rain crossed over to a large stand and picked up a crystal almost twelve inches in diameter, lifting the heavy jewel reverently.

When Rain turned back, Jonas stepped forward, his brows pinched. "Are you sure this is wise?"

"Of course I am." Rain sneered at the other man, stepping around him and depositing the crystal in the same spot where the chair had been. It hovered several feet off the ground, glittering in the light. "I've worked toward this moment for years. I won't let another Lockwood stop me. This time it will work. It's already working."

"But you said yourself the spell needs time to recharge! You just did the pull on Eben. You need to give it more time."

"I don't have more time!" Rain rounded on him, nostrils flaring. "That bitch took all my time! I have no choice. And it *will* work. It just might not be as stable as I'd hoped."

"Meaning what?" Jonas's voice was hard, and he moved back into Rain's path. "Will people die again?"

Rain stopped, his body growing stock-still. He tilted his head at Jonas. "They may. Why?"

Jae's father licked his lips, seeming to be fighting some internal battle. Finally, he squared his shoulders. "Then I can't let you do this. That was not what we agreed on."

A ghost of a smile flitted over Rain's lips. He chuckled, his raspy voice making it sound almost like a wheeze. "When will people realize they need to stop saying that to me?"

Jonas shook his head. "I'm sorry. I *am* on your side, Rain. We can find another way. We—"

"*There is no other way!*" Rain screamed, spittle flying from his mouth. His hands flew to Jonas's neck. Jonas jerked back, but he was too late. Electric white light burst from Rain's thin fingers as he squeezed.

I drew back behind the pillar, not wanting to witness what came next. I wasn't sorry the world would be rid of Jonas, even if he had tried to do one semi-decent thing in the end. And I was relieved in a way that Jae wouldn't have to be the one to kill him. But as much as I hated the man, his resemblance to Jae made my heart hurt. I couldn't watch his death.

A moment later, Ivy's soft, sad voice came in my ear. "It's over."

Heart thundering in my chest, I peeked back out into the room. Rain dropped Jonas's limp body. Small streaks of blood trailed from the dead man's eyes. The savagery that had overtaken Rain's face a moment ago faded, and he brushed his hands off on his suit jacket.

"There really is no other way," he said softly, seeming almost apologetic.

Gods, this guy is fucking insane.

And he was about to unleash the Great Death all over again, leaving an untold number of Gifted and Touched people dead or brain-dead while he rose to almost godlike power.

Whispering softly to himself, Rain fetched a large vial from a work table near the wall and walked back over to his machine. He uncorked the bottle and poured its contents over the crystal. The liquid was viscous and almost clear, running slowly down over each facet of the crystal, coating the entire thing.

He stepped back, raising his hands toward the large metal pieces of his machine. Lightning flared from his palms, but before he could unleash it, I dashed out from behind the pillar.

Twin flames burst from my hands, flying toward his back.

He spun, expanding the electricity between his hands to create a shield. My fireballs slammed into it and exploded in a burst of light.

Rain's lips pulled back from his teeth in a horrible impression of a smile. "Decided to come out of hiding, did you, Miss Lockwood? I suppose that makes you braver than your father. He tried to sneak past me, to destroy my life's work without even having the decency to look me in the eye first."

"Yeah, because you're the best judge of decency," I shot back, letting my invisibility illusion drop. It obviously hadn't stopped him from seeing me, and although it didn't take much energy to maintain, I needed to save every bit of power I had left.

Rain must've read my thoughts, because the bags under his eyes crinkled as he smirked. "Tired?"

"No." I glared at him, trying to form some plan of attack. I wouldn't stand a chance against him toe-to-toe, so I needed to find some way to surprise him, to put him off balance.

"Liar." He raised his hands, looking almost euphoric as a web of lightning surrounded his body, encasing him in a protective shell. The flaming sword appeared in his hands again, making him look like some kind of vengeful angel. "You should try power, Miss Lockwood. There's really nothing quite like it."

His glowing, electrified form advanced toward me.

CHAPTER 25

IT TOOK everything I had not to turn tail and run.

I'd never been afraid of a fight—but I'd never fought a glowing white monster with a blade made of fire before.

Pivoting, I threw a burst of flame toward the goo-covered crystal in the middle of the room. But Rain swung his sword in a wide arc, and my fire veered off course, careening toward his weapon. The sword absorbed the flickering orange light, pulsing as it seemed to glow even brighter.

Oh, for fuck's sake.

With a growl of frustration, I reached out with my magic, trying to move the crystal through levitation. It wouldn't budge. Rain advanced toward me, sword raised. I shot a spear of ice toward him, but he cleaved through it, the heat of the blade reducing the weapon to mist.

He lunged toward me, stabbing for my abdomen, and I jumped back. I avoided the strike by several inches, but sweat broke out on my brow at the blazing inferno of heat the weapon radiated.

Breath heaving, I forced a blast of air toward Rain, driving him backward. He let the lightning shield drop before he slammed into the base of his machine, the sword disappearing from his hands.

Ha! He didn't want to risk damaging his precious contraption.

Taking advantage of that weakness, I pressed forward, using the wind to keep him pinned. I threw a dagger at him, and it crossed into the path of the wind as it flew toward him. The gust sped it up but knocked it off course too. The blade clipped his arm, tearing a hole in his suit. Blood welled, staining the dark gray fabric a reddish-black.

The wind weakened as my strength ebbed, and Rain ducked to the side. I drew my other blade, heart thrumming so fast I couldn't distinguish the individual beats. Rain summoned his sword again, swinging wildly as he stepped forward. I raised my blade to block his, but as soon as they connected, the metal of my dagger began to melt. Globs of hot steel fell on my forearm, and I screamed in pain, dropping the handle.

His blade continued its arc, and I twisted, falling to the floor.

I had no more means to block his sword. My feet scrabbled against the smooth stone floor as I pushed myself away from him on my back. I felt for my thigh sheaths, desperate for any kind of weapon. One, at least, wouldn't be coming back at all. Where was the other?

Desperate, I shot a ball of fire at him, but the flame was weak. His sword gobbled it up immediately, pulsing with power.

Godsdamn it. Everything I did seemed to make him stronger.

In another two steps, he stood above me, his face a mask of triumph. For the second time today, he raised his sword for the killing strike.

Cold steel met my fingertips, and I could've wept for joy. My dagger.

As Rain raised his flaming blade high in both hands, I sat up quickly, yanking the dagger from its sheath. In one smooth motion, I plunged it into his gut, twisting as hard as I could.

His eyes went wide. A small grunt of pain and surprise escaped him.

Then he brought his own sword down.

The blade pierced my midsection, forcing me back down. Pain beyond anything I'd ever felt tore through my body as the blade both cut and burned. I screamed, my vocal cords shredding with the agony of the sound. He pulled the sword roughly out of my belly, and a new kind of pain flooded me.

Something hot and wet spread beneath my body.

I couldn't sit up.

I could only turn my head weakly to the side as Rain stumbled away from me. His sword sizzled, wet with my blood. He banished it with a flick of his wrist and used both hands to pull the dagger out of his stomach.

Fuck. It wasn't fair. We'd both landed a blow, but one of us had used a fucking sword made of fire.

And one of us still had power to spare.

As I watched through half-lidded eyes, Rain cupped his hands over his stomach, a bright glow emanating from his palms. The blood that was welling through his fingers slowed and finally stopped.

Keeping one hand on his stomach and walking with a hunched gait, Rain crossed to the door. He pushed it shut before waving a hand at the large chair Eben had once occupied. The chair floated over, and he wedged it in front of the door.

Straightening, but still breathing hard, Rain crossed back to the large machine in the middle of the room. He checked the crystal, hovering his hand over it and whispering to himself again. When he was satisfied, he stepped back two paces. Raising both hands, he sent small streams of electricity into the joints of the machine, his muttered whispers growing louder.

With a metallic whine, the pieces of the machine began to move, spinning and whirling at different speeds. A low *whump, whump, whump* sound filled the space.

Blackness edged my vision, so it took me a moment to realize what I was seeing. The night sky above the hole in the dome wavered, like the horizon on a hot day. That same wavering distortion filtered down toward the crystal, almost imperceptible.

The stone glowed, refracting light through the potion coating it and sending beautiful patterns all around the room. Then the beams of light suddenly merged into one. Pure magic streamed out from the crystal to join the small sphere of power suspended inside the whirring metal orb. It pulsed and grew slightly.

Swallowing was difficult. Breathing was difficult. But I couldn't tear my gaze away from the incredible, horrifying sight of magic being collected like water through a straw.

Rain's voice reached a fever pitch, his words loud and fast. As he spoke, he slowly walked around the machine. Then he stepped directly into the beam of magic transferring from the crystal to the ball inside the spinning metal arms.

His body jerked, his words cutting off, and for a moment I thought something had gone wrong.

Maybe the magic wasn't accessible to him this time either?

Then he laughed, holding his hands out to the side. Light emanated from his body, glowing from his eyes and even his mouth. As if he'd swallowed a star.

It had worked. Rain was pulling magic from the world and transferring it to himself. He would become as powerful as a god —and regardless of whether those who lost their magic survived the pull, their lives would be forfeit anyway.

I let my eyes drift shut, almost beyond caring as a bone-deep weariness tugged at me. We had tried. We had failed. I just wished death would hurry up and take me so I wouldn't have to listen to Rain's awful, raspy laugh anymore.

Gray eyes.

My father's eyes. Full of hope and love.

My grandmother's eyes. Glistening with understanding.

Beautiful green eyes, so full of emotion I could spend my life staring into them and never get enough. Sweet blue eyes that shone with kindness and laughter. Brown eyes like melted chocolate, warm and happy. And eyes so dark they were almost black, beckoning me to fall deeper into their swirling depths.

So many people had already died because of Rain. He'd taken my family from me. I wouldn't let him take my four too. I wouldn't let him destroy any more families.

The small pilot light of magic still burned inside me, guttering as my life force slowly dwindled. I had tried every kind of magic I could think of against Rain.

Except one.

Jae had told me in our lessons that a mage of my power should be able to access and control all four elements. But we'd never gotten to earth.

"Ivy?" My voice was faint and rough. I wasn't sure she could hear me over the noise of the machine.

But a moment later, her face appeared above mine. I could see her better now, and I wondered fleetingly if it was because she'd made herself more opaque again or if it was just because I was dying.

"What? What can I do?" Her hands fluttered over me, as if she wanted to touch my body, to try to heal me. But of course she couldn't.

"I need you to do something for me," I whispered. "Go back to the main level. Tell everyone to get out."

Her brow furrowed. "But what about you?"

"I have to finish something here. Tell them I'll be... I'll be right behind them." The lie tasted like ash on my tongue, but I needed to say it. They'd never leave without me otherwise. "They have transport spells. Tell them to get out of the tunnels. Off the mountain."

Speaking was becoming increasingly difficult. So was breathing.

I needed to save whatever strength I had left for what I planned to do next, so I stopped talking and just gazed up at Ivy, a silent plea in my eyes. The ghost was no stranger to death, and I knew she saw it on my face. Tears shimmered on her translucent cheeks, but she nodded.

"I'll tell them." She hesitated, her big brown eyes brimming with sadness. "I don't want you to die, Lana. Not even if you become a ghost."

Oddly touched by her sentiment, I smiled softly. "Don't worry. I'll be okay."

Another lie, but this one contained a kernel of truth. I wouldn't live through this, but if the last thing I saw in this world was Rain's machine collapsing, I *would* be okay.

The ghost rose slowly, smoothing her dress. With one last look down at me, she squared her shoulders and walked quickly through the barricaded door.

I turned my attention to Rain. Magic continued to pour in through the opening in the ceiling and filter through the crystal, and he still stood directly in the beam's path. His head was tilted back, and he no longer seemed aware of my presence—or anything at all, really. He was high on the power filling his body, on the magic running through his veins.

Letting my eyes drift shut, I extended my focus out around me. The floor in this room was smooth and polished, but it was still made out of stone. Just like the walls and ceilings were. I was surrounded by it.

Jae had never taught me how to use earth magic. Flame, I understood. It burned hot and bright, there in a flash and gone the next. Water and wind were more difficult for me. They both felt ephemeral, delicate—although their delicacy was an illusion. But what was earth?

Earth was solid.

Earth was stubborn.

It didn't negotiate, and it didn't ask permission.

The corner of my lip twitched. *Maybe earth* is *my element.*

I let my magic spread in tendrils through the rock and dirt beneath me then up through the walls and into the ceiling above.

Then I pulled.

The stone resisted at first. It was bound fast, settled in place by eons of pressure. My power strained and my whole body tensed, causing agony to flare in my stomach. I released the pull, breathing hard. Gritting my teeth, I sent my magic out again, but instead of trying to rip the stones apart, I sent a shock of vibration through them.

The floor rumbled, shaking beneath me.

A moment later, a crack appeared in one wall, running up toward the ceiling like a seam opening on a too-tight dress.

I pushed the magic harder, increasing the vibrations. More cracks appeared, and with a loud grating sound, a chunk of the ceiling collapsed. It hit the floor and exploded, breaking into smaller pieces of rock that flew across the room like missiles.

Another piece of the ceiling caved in, and this one hit the whirling metal arms of Rain's machine. With a grinding noise, they stopped spinning as the metal bent and contorted. Magic stopped filtering in from above, and when the flow from the crystal ebbed, Rain blinked slowly.

His glowing eyes turned to the broken piece of machinery, and then to me. Rage contorted his features as he raised his hands.

All the muscles in my body strained.

Please gods! End this now.

With a final push, I shoved every last bit of strength and magic I had into the earth around me. A jagged spike thrust up from the rock in front of Rain, piercing his body and lifting him off his feet as it grew upward. His eyes widened in shock and pain, and electric magic flared at his fingertips.

Then, with an ear-splitting crack, another piece of the ceiling collapsed. Rain didn't even have a chance to look up before it came down on him, crushing him and the crystal beneath its heavy weight.

There was a bright flash of light, and I turned my face away.

A second flash came, blinding in its intensity. The world went white, even through my closed eyelids.

As the flare of light faded, darkness fell.

The rumbling grew louder around me.

My magic was tapped out; I was no longer using it to disrupt the stone.

But the earth was stubborn. I'd started something, and it was damned well going to finish it.

Through the exhaustion and pain, through the roaring in my ears, I thought I heard someone calling my name.

Then I didn't hear anything at all.

CHAPTER 26

Blackness.

Silence.

It was peaceful here, in this empty space where I floated.

My body didn't ache, and exhaustion no longer hung on me.

Slowly, I drifted downward like a feather, finally settling on a soft, smooth surface.

Warm breath tickled my ear. A large hand rested across my stomach, another on my ribcage. Muscled bodies pressed close to me, encasing me in a protective shell.

If this is death, it's not so bad.

But it couldn't be death. I felt far too solid for that.

I gradually became aware of my own deep breathing, the weight of my eyelids, and the soreness of my muscles. But most notable was the absence of pain in my abdomen.

Swallowing roughly, I tried out my vocal chords, murmuring a soft, unintelligible noise.

The breath at my ear stopped. The hands and bodies pulled away from me.

Well, fuck. If I'd known that was going to happen, I never would've made a peep.

I mumbled again in protest at the loss, shifting restlessly. My body still didn't feel quite like my own, and when I ordered my eyelids to open, they flat-out refused.

"Killer? Oh, thank fuck!"

Fen.

I tried again to force my eyes open, my hand groping for him blindly. He caught it, raising it to his lips. He rubbed his nose across my knuckles, inhaling the scent of my skin.

Then suddenly, all their hands were on me again. A face pressed to my stomach, warm lips touched my forehead, and cool fingers traveled up my legs. The overload of sensations made me gasp, and my eyes finally flew open.

Four faces peered down at me. My favorite faces in the entire world.

"Godsdamn it, Lana! Don't ever fucking scare us like that again!" Corin's voice was too full of relief for his words to have much bite, and he buried his face in my stomach again, as if he could somehow meld us into one being.

Akio leaned against the headboard of the large bed in my room in Beatrice's house. He brushed my hair away from my face, his dark eyes gleaming. "Welcome back, kitten."

Jae kneeled by my feet, his hands tracing patterns over my legs, leaving goose bumps in their wake. His elegant features were tight, like he couldn't quite trust what he was seeing yet.

"We thought we lost you," he murmured, his grip tightening on my thigh.

"I…" I cleared my throat and tried again, my voice scratchy. "I thought you did too." A sudden panic rose in my chest. I hadn't just imagined it, had I? Gone into some kind of vivid hallucination brought on by shock and blood loss? "Rain! Is he—?"

"He's dead." Fen grinned at me, though his chocolate eyes were shadowed. "You did it, killer. You stopped him."

Relief flooded me. "I used earth magic. I tore the place down. Did everyone get out? I told Ivy to warn you."

The wolf shifter's expression darkened. "Oh, she delivered your message, all right. Then after we told her where she could shove it, she agreed to bring us to you."

"It didn't take much convincing, actually. I don't think she liked your plan any better than we did." Akio arched a brow at me.

I sat up slowly, taking my time so I could let the world stop spinning. "It wasn't so much a plan as a last ditch effort. It was my only option. Rain had started the magic pull."

Jae nodded solemnly. "We know."

My head whipped toward him, the sudden movement blurring my vision again. "How? Did it take your magic? Did it kill people?"

"No one died. But we learned after the fact that several people were almost entirely drained. Then there were two huge pulses of magic, and the pull stopped."

"I tried to stop him from turning it on," I murmured. "But he was more powerful than me. I couldn't fight anymore. He…."

My hand went to my stomach. I was wearing a soft gray T-shirt and a pair of pajama pants. I lifted the tee, staring down at the large pink scar trailing across my abdomen. Even though it was healed, the sight of the thick line brought back a stab of remembered pain. That had been a killing blow.

I bit my lip, looking up at Jae. "Thank you for healing me."

"Actually," he said, a smile ghosting across his face, "it wasn't just me."

My brow furrowed. "Then who...?"

Fen reached around me to punch Corin in the arm, grinning ear-to-ear. I turned to the blond man, eyes widening, and he ran a hand through his hair, a flush rising in his cheeks.

"*You?*"

He shrugged. "Jae had used so much magic already—in the fight, and to keep the ceiling from collapsing on us while we tried to get to you. Once we finally found you, we used a transport spell to get out. But you were in bad shape. Jae tried to heal you, but you were slipping away."

I reached out to grip his hand, and he squeezed mine tightly.

"I couldn't lose you, Lana. I put my hands on you, not even knowing what I was trying to do, just wanting more than anything to keep you here with us. Light burst out of my palms and poured into you, and your wounds finally started to close."

"Corin." I stared at him, touched and awed. "How...?"

He looked down. "I went to talk to Asprix after everything settled down. He's pretty fascinated by all of us now. I think if we let him, he'd lock us up in a room and study us for days."

I chuckled, relieved to hear that the old reader had survived the fight. "Yeah, not gonna happen."

"I told him you'd say that." One side of Corin's mouth lifted in a grin before he grew serious again. "He did find a small amount of magic inside me. Don't get too excited; I'm not Gifted or anything. It's probably yours, from the bond. I was only able to access it because of how badly I needed it in that moment. I forced it to act."

"That's incredible," I breathed, then tugged his hand to make him look at me. "I knew you'd always protect me."

He smiled, but his grip on my hand didn't loosen. We had come so close to losing each other. It would take some time for that fear to pass.

I glanced around at the rest of my four. "Was Olene there? Or did I imagine that?"

Jae shook his head. "No, she was there. Noble brought her."

"How? Why?"

"Their attack on the palace was more difficult than expected. More Gifted had joined Rain's ranks than we'd hoped. Olene went into hiding after he killed Theron, but when word of the attack on the palace got out, she came to help."

My eyes bugged out of my head. "Representative Romo came to help the *Blighted* take the People's Palace?"

"Well, I think it was more that she came to help anybody trying to unseat Rain." Fen chuckled. "But the end result was pretty much the same. Once he realized Rain had come after us, Noble brought her to Rain's lair."

My stomach twisted, remembering the sight of her lying unconscious on the ground. "Did she survive the fight?"

"Yes. She took a bad hit, but it didn't kill her. When Ivy came to warn us, Noble got her out with a transport spell." Akio slipped off the bed, coming around the side to stand over us all.

"And is she... *still* alive?"

"Of course, kitten. She's been granted amnesty by the Resistance in exchange for her continued help. Several other Gifted officials were captured in the fight, but believe it or not, Noble isn't big on public executions."

I grimaced. "Yeah. Me neither."

Faint voices filtered in through the door, drawing my attention.

"Speaking of…" Jae lifted a brow. "That's probably him. He usually comes by about this time of day."

His words pricked at a question that had been lingering in my mind. "Usually? How long was I out?"

"Three days." Akio crossed his tattooed arms over his chest. He was predictably shirtless again, but I didn't mind. In fact, I was seriously considering seeing if I could get him to agree to never wear a shirt again.

"Three *days*?" My eyes bugged. I let go of Corin and Fen's hands and scooted toward the edge of the bed.

Akio's palms dropped onto my shoulders the moment I stood, forcing me to plop back onto the soft mattress. "And where exactly do you think you're going, kitten?"

"Downstairs! Outside! To the palace!" I tried to rise again on each word, but he pushed me back down every time. We were both so stubborn we could probably do this all day.

When I moved to stand again, Fen wrapped his arms around me from behind, laughing. "It's okay, killer. There's lots to do, but we've got time. Thanks to you."

I sank back into his embrace, not wanting to admit that standing up that fast so many times had made my head spin. "Can I at least go downstairs? I want to see Noble."

They all shared a look, and I was already preparing my arguments when Jae nodded. "He wants to see you too."

He rose from the bed, offering me his arm. I took it gratefully. My legs felt jelly-like, and my muscles quivered slightly with the effort of holding me up. But mostly, I just wanted to be close to Jae, to feel his calming presence like a balm. He pressed a kiss to my temple before leading me toward the door.

As we walked slowly down the stairs, I shot a glance at him.

"Why was I out for so long? You and Corin healed me, right? So that should've been that."

"You almost completely drained your magic, Lana. I was exhausted after that fight, and I'm a highly trained mage. You'd never used anywhere near the amount of power you did that night, and when you brought down the cave walls… you were tapping into what was left of your life force along with your magic."

I blanched. "Shit. So I really am lucky to be alive."

"More than lucky." We hit the bottom step, and he turned to me, speaking softly. "There were two magical pulses right after you started tearing down the room. It was the magic Rain stole. The small amount he took this time, and everything he took the first time."

I gaped at him. "That's what those flashes of light were?"

"Yes. My best guess is that when you destroyed the machine, it released the magic he was currently drawing. And when that exploded, it disrupted the stabilized magic from his first pull."

"So… where is it now?"

He shrugged, gesturing to indicate the world at large. "Out there. We all felt the pulses of power. And Asprix can't verify this, but I believe they're what awakened the glimmer of magic inside Corin."

My mind reeled. But before I could formulate a response, I was wheeled around and pulled into an energetic embrace.

"Well done, Crow! Well fucking done!"

"Hey," Akio growled from the stairs behind us. "Be gentle. She just woke up."

"Oh come on, Akio!" Fen laughed, barreling down the steps. "Just because you're a delicate flower doesn't mean she is too. I bet she could kick your ass right now." He squeezed my shoulder

219

as he passed, leaning in to whisper in my ear, "*Are* you okay though?"

I nodded, holding back a laugh. He was just as overprotective as the others, but I appreciated that he at least pretended not to be. And I *could* kick Akio's ass. Maybe not right this second, but I had plans for the future that definitely involved slamming him into a wall... or the floor... or whatever furniture happened to be around.

Noble seemed to get the hint after even Jae gave him a threatening look. He pulled back and held me at arm's length, his already sharp features made even more angular by the wide smile that stretched across his face. His penetrating gaze took in my face, and behind the almost manic energy that always seemed to exude from him, I felt his concern.

"I'm fine, Noble. Really. What about you? You took the palace? Did we lose many people?"

Jae tugged me away from the Resistance leader and helped me into the large sitting room. I sank onto the couch gratefully. I was feeing more like myself with every passing minute, but it would be a while yet before I was up to full strength.

The rest of my four settled around me, and Noble followed us in, leaning over the back of one of the beautifully upholstered chairs.

He pursed his lips for a moment, his jaw tensing. "Our losses weren't catastrophic, but we did lose fighters. If Olene Romo hadn't shown up when she did, it would've been much worse."

Tears pricked my eyes, and I spoke around the lump in my throat. "I'm sorry, Noble. Gods, I hate this. So many lives, gone. It's such a waste."

He shook his head, his expression hard.

"No. Not a waste. Not if we don't let it become one." He paced away from the chair, his energy spiking again as his eyes lit with an inner fire. "I've been thinking a lot about that quote. 'To reap the harvest of perpetual peace, by this one bloody trial of sharp war.'"

"Yeah? What about it?" I tilted my head to the side, my pulse already quickening to match his fervent passion.

"We've been through the bloody trial. We fought the war. Now it's up to us to make sure those who fought didn't lose their lives in vain. We need to stop the cycle of hate and violence and start something new, something better." He rubbed the back of his neck, his wide smile breaking forth again. "It's not going to be easy. It's gonna be hard as hell. But I know we can do it."

CHAPTER 27

One Year Later

"So, what do you think?" Corin wrapped his arms around me from behind, and I dropped my head back against his chest, blinking away the tears blurring my eyes.

"I think... it's fucking beautiful."

The Pacific Ocean spread out before us, the cool blue water dyed orange and red by the rays of the setting sun. Soft waves rolled across the water, and the taste of salt lingered on my tongue. Gulls cried softly overhead, circling and wheeling through the air. My bare feet sank into the wet sand as foamy waves licked at my toes.

"Is it like you imagined it would be?" His voice was soft and warm in my ear.

"No," I whispered. "It's better."

A loud whoop caught my attention, and I laughed as Fen dove under a wave, popping up after it passed and shaking his shaggy brown hair out of his eyes. Jae waded through the shallow water nearby, his sleeves rolled up to his elbows and his pants rolled up to his knees. He looked casual and elegant, like a prince of the ocean out for a stroll in his domain. Next to us, Akio stood staring out over the water, lost in his own thoughts. His hand gripped mine though, our fingers laced tightly together.

The stunning beauty of the entire scene overwhelmed me, and I didn't want to blink, didn't want to miss even a half-second of it.

"Thank you for bringing me here." I snuggled back against Corin's body, the warmth of his embrace a delicious contrast to the chilly sea air.

"I've wanted to forever, Lana. Sorry we didn't see any jellyfish though." He chuckled.

"This is enough. This is more than enough."

He sighed contentedly, resting his hands on the small bump of my growing belly and sending a little thrill through me. That development was new enough I still felt a zing of pride and nerves every time I thought about it.

I'd never pictured myself as a mother, and I was a little terrified I'd be awful at it. But then again, I'd never pictured myself falling madly in love with four men either, and that had been the best thing that ever happened to me.

My four all liked to joke that it'd be easy enough when the baby came to guess which of them was the father based on what kind of powers it had. Fen's favorite comment was, "If it comes out howling, it's mine."

But the truth was, we might not ever know for sure.

Jae had been right about the two pulses of magic released the night I destroyed Rain's machine. They had awakened something.

Over the past year, numerous magical children had been born to nonmagical parents. Some people who'd spent their whole lives without magic suddenly began developing powers, and even those with magic started manifesting strange new abilities.

The world was changing. There were still plenty of people who didn't have any magic, but the lines were blurring—whether through marriage and birth or through the power that seemed to seep into people from the very air, the difference between *magic* and *nonmagic* became less and less distinct every day. The terms "Blighted," "Gifted," and "Touched" had fallen out of use too, remnants of an old system we were working hard to destroy.

Noble had adamantly resisted putting people to death in the aftermath of the fight against Rain, despite calls from some of the Blighted to do so. Gifted citizens who had helped Rain or done violence to the Blighted were given a trial, and punishments were handed down to fit their crimes—but there were no mass public executions. The world had seen enough of that for a long while.

And after the revelation of what Rain had done, many prominent magic users stepped forward to condemn the mistreatment of the Blighted and admit their complicity in not stopping it sooner. Too little, too late, I thought, but Noble accepted their penance gracefully, reminding them that they *were* complicit and it was now their duty to make it right.

There were still some magic users who would always insist on calling themselves Gifted. Those who would posture and claim superiority over anyone with no magic. But they were a dying breed, screaming pitifully as they faded away.

Noble was well suited to leadership, and maybe part of the reason for that was because he didn't cling to it. He'd led the new government long enough to let things stabilize, but our first public election in years would be held soon.

I snorted softly, remembering several of our most recent

conversations. Despite months of subtle and not-so-subtle hints from him, I had adamantly refused to run for office.

I'd come to accept what Akio told me that day—I *was* a leader, whether I wanted to be or not. But I had no interest in running a government. I'd rather get my hands dirty with work, helping tear down the wall that separated the Outskirts from the Capital or repairing the neglected areas of the city as an influx of people arrived from the now-disbanded Blighted encampments. In other cities as well, walls were being torn down and city-centers expanded as more people arrived.

The last year hadn't been easy. There was so much to do.

Some days it seemed like an impossible task.

And some days it felt like the country balanced on a knife's edge, on the precipice of slipping over into chaos and violence again.

But we wouldn't let it.

Noble was right. We had fought hard to get where we were. And like good farmers, we would plant the seeds, tend our crops, and keep the predators at bay so we—and the generations to come—could reap the harvest of peace.

Corin gave me a little squeeze, and I jumped. I'd gotten lost in my thoughts when I meant to be soaking up the scene around me.

"Look at you two." He laughed, swiveling his head between Akio and me. "If you both stared any harder, you'd probably set the ocean on fire."

Akio rolled his eyes, the red glow of the sun highlighting his sharp features. "We're both highly intelligent people. We have a lot to think about."

That just made Corin laugh harder, and I elbowed him in the ribs.

He pressed a kiss to my hair and released me, still chuckling under his breath.

I stepped toward Akio, pulling my hand from his so I could wrap my arms around his waist.

Worry twisted my gut for a moment as I pressed my head to his chest, listening to his strong heartbeat.

I could guess what he'd been thinking about.

A few weeks ago, we'd gone to see Asprix again. The old reader really was obsessed with us, and not just because Corin still brought him a tincture for his back. He'd done a reading on all five of us, and then shocked the hell out of me by informing us that the bond between us had made Akio mortal.

I'd spent days agonizing over the revelation and despising the bond all over again. Akio had finally found me up in the study on the third floor and demanded to know what my problem was. I'd been certain he would hate me for taking his immortality, but instead, he kissed me until I saw stars then hauled me off the couch and fucked me on the desk.

As we lay in each other's arms afterward, he'd murmured softly in my ear, "I would choose a mortal life with you over eternity any day."

Of course, the next day he'd found a single gray hair on his head and completely lost his shit. I'd promised him it was just a fluke, and that I would love him even more when we were old and gray. And besides, Asprix also mentioned it was likely all five of us would live a long, long time—a remnant of Akio's demon immortality passed on to all of us.

Tilting my head, I gazed into the incubus's impossibly beautiful eyes. "Good thoughts, I hope."

He looked down at me, his full lips curving into a sinful grin. "Kitten, when they're of you, they're always *bad*."

I slapped his hard stomach playfully, even as a flush of warmth filled my body at his smooth, teasing tone. The nails of my other hand dug into his back for a moment, just to remind him who he was playing with. The low growl that rumbled in his chest assured me he did.

"Wet wolf, comin' through!"

Fen sloshed out of the water and sprinted up the shore toward us, plucking me from Akio's embrace and spinning me around, water flying from us like a sprinkler. The entire front of my body was wet when he finally released me, and I was breathless with laughter.

"Well done, Fen." Jae smiled as he approached, humor glinting in his eyes. "I'm sure Lana was hoping to find a way to get soaking wet *without* going in the ocean."

"Well, if she's looking for a way to get soaking wet, I can definitely help her with that." Fen waggled his eyebrows at me, adding two wet handprints to my waist as he pulled me in for a kiss that made my knees soften.

I'd long since given up feeling awkward about what we all shared. To the rest of the world, I was still The Crow, an almost mythical, larger-than-life figure who'd helped bring down a genocidal maniac and uncover the greatest lie in our collective history. The bond between me and my four was just one more part of the legend surrounding us, and I was happy to leave it at that.

Besides, it really wasn't anybody's business but ours.

Fen pecked me on the lips again before darting up the beach to fetch his clothes. Sand was already collecting on his legs, and I grimaced. Retta was *not* going to be happy if he tracked that through the house. She'd probably tell Darcy to stop making his favorite bread for a week.

227

They'd both insisted on staying on, and I hadn't had the slightest inclination to stop them. With the money I'd inherited from Beatrice, I paid them enough that they wouldn't have to work at all after a few years. But even then, I hoped they'd stay with us. The house wouldn't be the same without them and their families in it.

Jae ran a finger down my wet shirt, tracing a path between my breasts to my belly. His eyes heated, but he pursed his lips in concern. "We should get back. I don't want you in wet clothes for too long."

"Okay. Just one more minute."

I turned back toward the water as Jae pulled a transport spell out of his pocket. I lifted my nose into the air and inhaled deeply, trying to absorb the tangy breeze so I could carry it back home with me.

"We can come back, kitten," Akio murmured softly. "Tomorrow, and the next day, and the next day if we want. We have the rest of our lives."

I glanced up at him, the pleasant shiver at the realization enhanced by the fact that it was Akio who'd pointed it out to me.

He was right. Our long lives stretched out ahead of us like the ocean, full of endless possibilities and unknown adventures.

Our story wasn't over.

It was just beginning.

THANK YOU FOR READING!

Thank you so much for reading *Consort of Rebels* and going on this journey with Lana and her men!

If you're hungry for more, I'm currently working on two other reverse harem series, *Her Soulkeepers* and *The Vampires' Fae*, which will release in early 2019.

In the meantime, you can keep the adventure going with a free copy of *Kissed by Shadows*, a prequel novella that has more of Corin and Lana's backstory.

Join my mailing list at www.sadiemossauthor.com/subscribe, and I'll send you your FREE copy!

MESSAGE TO THE READER

Please consider leaving a review! Honest reviews help indie authors like me connect with awesome readers like you. It is truly one of the best ways you can help support an author whose work you enjoy!

If you liked this book, I would be forever grateful if you'd take a minute to leave a review (it can be as short or long as you like) on my book's Amazon page.

Thank you so much!

ACKNOWLEDGMENTS

First and foremost, thank you to my incredible husband and my sweet puppy for putting up with all my mad ramblings about the *Magic Awakened* series.

Thank you, Jacqueline Sweet, for the amazing cover! I love what you've created for this series.

To my amazing beta readers: thank you, thank you, thank you!

ABOUT THE AUTHOR

Sadie Moss is obsessed with books, craft beer, and the supernatural. She has often been accused of living in a world of her own imagination, so she decided to put those worlds into books.

When Sadie isn't working on her next novel, she loves spending time with her adorable puppy, binge-watching comedies on Hulu, and hanging out with her family.

She loves to hear from her readers, so feel free to say hello at sadiemoss.author@gmail.com.

And if you want to keep up with her latest news and happenings, you can like her Facebook page, or follow her on Twitter, Goodreads, and Amazon.

Made in the USA
Monee, IL
25 November 2019